F.B.I. SPECIAL AGENT

Cheyenne Charlie, Native American law student turned G-Man, is one of the Bureau's top agents. The New York office sends for him to investigate a sinister criminal gang called the Blond Boys. Their getaway cars somehow disappear in well-lit streets; they jam police radios; and now they've begun to add brutal murder to their daring robberies. Cheyenne follows a tangled trail that leads him to a desperate fight to the death in the beautiful scenery of the Catskill Mountains . . .

GORDON LANDSBOROUGH

F.B.I.
SPECIAL
AGENT

Complete and Unabridged

LINFORD
Leicester

First published in Great Britain

First Linford Edition
published 2009

British Library CIP Data

Landsborough, Gordon.
    F.B.I. special agent. - -
    (Linford mystery library)
    1. United States. Federal Bureau of
    Investigation- -Officials and employees- -
    Fiction. 2. Government investigators- -
    United States- -Fiction. 3. Gangs- -
    New York (State)- -New York- -Fiction.
    4. Suspense fiction. 5. Large type books.
    I. Title II. Series
    823.9'14–dc22

    ISBN 978–1–84782–940–5

Published by
F. A. Thorpe (Publishing)
Anstey, Leicestershire

Set by Words & Graphics Ltd.
Anstey, Leicestershire
Printed and bound in Great Britain by
T. J. International Ltd., Padstow, Cornwall

This book is printed on acid-free paper

1

Letter of death

A man came softly down the stairs. He was a little runt of a fellow, and his legs stuck out as thin as matches under the worn bottoms of his pants. The door that had started to open on the drab, dull landing stopped moving.

There was a woman washing the worn steps, it sometimes happened that someone got around to cleaning the place. She was not young but not as old as a work-weary life made her appear now. She soaped and slopped slowly, as if the effort were infinite labour. She had hair that was as ragged as the cloth in her hand, and her skin had the greyness of the water in the bucket.

But all the same, she wasn't doing harm to anyone.

She didn't hear the skinny little runt come down the stairs. He came quickly, softly, not wanting her to hear. There was an expression of anticipation on his thin, sallow face, and his mouth was puckered up as if he were sucking in his breath. His small, brown eyes, that had the quick brightness of a mouse's, were on those roughened, water-wrinkled fingers, where she rested on her left hand.

He came down the last three steps in a swift rush.

His right foot came up, and then stabbed down, and even before the heel made contact a flame of joy suffused that thin face.

The heel ground on to those fingers.

The woman screamed in agony, and her bucket went flying in a mess of water down the stairs as she lashed out with her scrubbing hand to stop the awful pain of the other.

At once the runt jumped down the last steps, then backed defensively against the wall in the passage. It wasn't easy to see his face in the light there, but to that other man it was apparent . . . the sadistic joy at sight of the woman's suffering.

The runt said, swiftly, 'I didn't see you.

This landing should be better lit. You should have heard me an' got outa the way.' Anything except admit the truth. That he'd wanted to hurt those fingers the moment he saw them below him.

The woman moaned and clutched her hand. She rose unsteadily to her feet and said, 'Mother of God how it hurts! Mother of God, do I always have to suffer!'

The runt was backing. His head was lowered a little, and his brown, mouse-eyes were watching with nervous intensity. The door began to open slowly.

The runt said, 'I'd give you something for that, only I ain't got nothin'.'

The woman settled slowly on the second step and bent her head in anguish. When she looked up again the cause of her suffering had gone. Yet her head had been lowered for less time than it required for a man to have continued the several more flights down to the street level.

The runt had been backing down the unlit passage, when fingers came slowly around the back of his neck. They were

3

very strong fingers, and they gripped with an intensity that conveyed a warning . . . that a neck might break if there were resistance. The runt's neck.

He found himself being drawn inside a room, and saw the door close on the passage as he was being turned. Then the grip was released on his neck.

It was like any other room in that apartment house. It wasn't big, it wasn't furnished worth calling the name, and it wasn't the sort of place that any man would want to call 'home'. But it was home to the man with the strong fingers.

The put-up bed let into the wall hadn't gone right back, and there was a brown end of a blanket dangling. On a rickety side table were the remains of a meal . . . a badly hacked loaf of bread, a scrape of butter, and some canned meat that the flies were liking a lot.

The room looked more than usually uninviting because of the appalling litter . . . a lot of radio stuff on a table by the window, and a mess of thin pieces of leather all over the floor.

The runt looked at the man. He was

formless, balding, bespectacled. As unhealthy looking as a thing that crawls into deeper slime when a rotting log is disturbed.

There was soft fat all over his round head and sagging body. The fat that comes to a man who sits all day at a desk or a workbench and shuns exercise like some people avoid water. And his height was lost in a stoop that spoke yet again of years of slouching over a desk, and there was a pallor on his face that said it was no friend of the sun and even of daylight.

And those short-sighted, peering eyes told the story of book-poring after midnight with insufficient light to read by.

But his hands were strong.

They were the hands of a man who is used to gripping tools, and they were bigger than usual, and the skin was calloused and roughened from work. They were in contrast to the softness of every other part of him.

The runt was up against the wall, his bright brown eyes watching. Most of his life the runt had been standing defensively up against walls, alert for danger from bigger, stronger inhabitants of New

York City. And from cops.

The pallid, stooping slug of a man peered close to his face, and when he spoke his voice seemed jerky and uncertain and nervous.

He said, 'I saw you come down the stairs. I was watching your face. You did that on purpose.'

The runt said, quickly, 'As God's my judge . . . '

'He isn't. Or he wouldn't have let you do that. You did it because it's your nature to like hurting people, isn't it?' The unhealthy slug sighed and eased the spectacles on his formless nose. 'Most people seem to like hurting others. Most people like to hurt me when they see me. I get hurt all the time. You wouldn't know why, would you?'

His head was moving in questing little circles, as though even from a range of two feet he had difficulty in seeing the runt's face clearly.

The runt, getting over the shock of being gripped so roughly by the neck, licked his lips and came away from the wall an inch or two. He said, 'Maybe I

6

could guess,' and he made it sound insulting. He wasn't afraid of this slug any more, and you can hurt ... and enjoy hurting ... verbally just as much as you can hurt physically. 'You look like you're made to take punishment, brother. Next time, just leave my neck alone, an' let me go on my way.'

He reached out for the door handle. When he turned his eyes back to the slug he saw something that stopped him from going out.

There was a roll of dough in the slug's hands, so big it looked the size of a Florida cabbage. The runt's immediate thought was: What the hell, all that dough an' he stops in a crummy joint! This guy ain't on the up-an'-up!

And that encouraged and emboldened him still further. He felt at home among guys who weren't on the up-and-up. He tarried at the door, his thin, sallow face looking steadily at that roll.

The slug said, 'I was just goin' out to ask that woman to do a job for me. I heard you say you hadn't got nothin'. Maybe you could do this job for me ...

that woman wouldn't have been so good, anyway.' When the slug spoke his words came uneasily, as if all his thoughts were crowded with uncertainty, and there was a quaver in his voice that seemed like a tremble of fear.

But what had he got to be afraid of? The runt thought: Jeez, how come a guy like this gets hisself a roll of lettuce so big? It ain't natural. It ain't right!

Aloud he said, 'If there's enough money in it, maybe I could at that.' He never took his eyes off that roll.

The slug got a little courage at that and said, 'Tell me who you are, and what you were doing in this house. You don't live here.'

The runt let his quick brown eyes travel slowly up to that dead-white, flabby face. Then he told the truth, and because he resorted to such an unusual practice he again showed his contempt for the creature before him.

'I was casin' the joint. I got a lotta room in my pocket these days, an' I thought to pick somep'n up that might fill 'em.' Disgust edged his words. 'The hell, the only room that didn't have a locked door didn't have nothin' in it but mops and brushes.'

'You didn't have any luck?' And the slug was nodding in satisfaction, as if everything the runt was saying pleased him. As the runt had guessed it might because of the size of that roll in his hand.

The runt's eyes were back on the lettuce. He was saying to himself: No guy can have so many small notes an' be honest. Must be he robs banks, but he don't look like it.

And with that thought he was dead right about the slug.

'What's your name?' That quavering, uncertain voice.

The runt stirred. 'You won't believe it, brother. It's Gue. Hickman Gue. So help me, that's the truth of it. Guess my old man didn't like me none, else how can you account for it?'

The slug said, 'I'm Gell.' And then he stopped, so quickly that Hicky Gue knew he hadn't intended to give his real name and it had slipped out and now he was regretting it.

Hicky Gue wrinkled his long, mouse-like nose. 'Gell? I've seen that name somewhere. What's your other name, brother? Come clean, you might as well.'

Gell's face quivered in a fat sigh. He blinked rapidly and nervously and then said, 'It's Joe Gell.'

Hicky said, 'Joe Gell?' He made a sudden gesture of impatience with his long, thin fingers. 'Of course. Now I remember where I've seen it.' And then he looked round the disorderly room again and thought: What'n hell's Joe Gell up to, in this place? For the Joe Gell whose name he had seen so often should have had a sizable amount of money, and wasn't any crook to have to hide away in a crummy, downtown joint like this.

But Joe Gell wasn't telling him anything. Only how to earn some money. And good money, too.

'This little job. I'll give you fifty dollars for doin' it. You go to an address I'll give you, an' you ask for a letter addressed to Jay Gee, see? You don't come back with that letter. You just walk around with it for an hour or two, then you write my address . . . this one here . . . on the envelope and re-mail it. Get that? *And you don't ever come back to this apartment.* And you don't write to me, you don't phone me, and you don't tell anyone where I am. You understand?'

Excitement . . . or perhaps it was fear . . . gave a degree of firmness to his tone.

Hicky Gue said, carefully, 'You want me to re-mail a letter to you. You want it done this way so that no one'll ever be able to trace you through that letter. That's it, ain't it?'

Joe Gell's blank white face nodded uncertainly. 'That's about it.'

Hicky tried a long shot. He was good at long shots. 'It must be important to you, not lettin' someone get on your trail. That explains why you're in hidin' when you could afford the best place in town.' He looked back at that wad of greenbacks. 'It's worth more than fifty bucks,' he said suddenly, and he made his voice sound tough.

He got a surprise, then. Joe Gell just nodded. 'It's worth a lot more than fifty bucks to me. I'm prepared to pay you more, Hicky. A lot more. Keep your mouth shut, and a coupla weeks from now if I've not seen or heard from you and that letter comes safely to me, I'll send you . . . five hundred bucks.'

Hicky's small mouth came up in a suddenly widening 'O'. His eyes sought . . . and were reassured. The guy looked as if he meant what he said. Hicky thought: Gell's too soft, anyway, to try a double-cross. I know, now . . .

Gell's voice came up in an eager quaver . . . 'You give me your address, Hicky, then I c'n send you the money. Here's the address for you to get the letter. I want you to go right away, right now, see? An' here's fifty bucks for you.'

When Hicky had finished writing and the dollars were safely in his pockets, he said, abruptly, 'Why don't you go yourself? What's it about?' And he didn't expect the truth.

Joe Gell's fingers were playing absently with a variable condenser on the littered table. He was trying to think of a convincing lie. 'It's a girl . . . a woman.' With a shape like that it couldn't be a girl, Hicky thought cynically. It'd have to be a woman to take to a thing like Gell.

'I got in trouble with her husband,' Joe Gell mumbled, his face weaving about as be peered from one thing to another but not looking at Hicky. 'I think maybe he'll be watching for me where we get our letters sent.'

Hicky crossed to the door. 'You should take time off to rehearse your stories, Joe. That didn't sound good. Me, I c'n bring 'em out at a moment's notice an' they all sound brilliant.' As an afterthought, he added, 'Except to cops.'

They went out on to the passage. The woman was sitting on the steps. She was crying, only she was so dried up inside she had to do it without tears. She took a long time to do anything, even to stop crying.

She didn't say anything when Hicky came in sight again, but she went on making noises in her scrawny throat. So Hicky shuffled uncertainly, and then said, 'I got a dollar might cure that. I just come into dough.'

He gave her a dollar of the new roll. He

hated parting with it, but he thought: What the hell, I got forty-nine more, an' then there's five hundred to come in a coupla weeks. An' then . . .

Then Hicky Gue might have learned enough to start blackmailing the white-faced slug.

He turned away from the woman. The door was closed behind him. Joe Gell must have ducked back out of sight when he saw the woman sitting there. Hicky shrugged. 'Kinda retirin' personality,' he grinned and then he went down the stairs and he was whistling 'I Gotta Date with an Angel.' Which was prophetic, or optimistic, but no one will ever know.

He took the El to a point near the address he had been given. When he got off he found he was less than a block away. He walked it. It turned out to be a drab cigar store and hairdresser's.

The El ran right overhead. That would keep one hairdresser from talking Ezzard Charles and ball game while clipping locks, Hicky thought. It was a busy street, with mostly low, old buildings on either side. A dilapidated, down-at-heel quarter.

Near to the place he had to pass a police car. Hicky's eyes narrowed suspiciously when he saw it. He trusted no man . . . nothing. And he wasn't going to walk into any police trap. So he stood around and watched until he was reassured.

That cop car had nothing to do with that hairdresser's, in time he felt certain. They'd got hold of a motorist and they were giving him hell, and it was no playacting. Cops are too dumb to playact. He was a little fellar, that motorist, and he was getting smaller and smaller as they shouted at him. You'd have thought he'd committed murder, but Hicky knew he'd only gone across a red light or parked up against a fire plug or something like that. They were big cops and he was a little fellar, and that explained everything to Hicky. Big fellars like to pitch into runts . . .

He cased that street pretty thoroughly, walked past the hairdresser's four or five times, before he decided to go in. But there was nothing suspicious about that street. Just a few cars parked and a lot of people going about their business. And everybody shouting because you had to shout because of that roaring el overhead.

A thin, lined, grey-headed man with steel-rimmed, army-issue glasses came out through a glass door when he entered the overcrowded shop. He was carrying a comb and a pair of scissors, and there was hair clinging to his white, knee-length jacket. Gue guessed he was the proprietor.

His face twitched into an unconvincing salesman's smile. 'Sir, I'm jes' waitin' to serve you.' Times had changed since the war years when people at home made so much money they didn't give a damn for anyone not even customers. Hicky reflected on the change. He should have known. He'd been no nearer the European fighting than Coney Island, and no nearer Japan than Ossining, which common people referred to as Sing-Sing.

Hicky said, 'Then serve me any letters addressed to Jay Gee.' He passed the receipt across.

The hairdresser looked over the top of his glasses at Hicky, then down to the receipt. He said, shortly, 'You ain't the guy that came first time an' registered. He was fat.'

'He sent me. He couldn't come himself.' Hicky was alert and suspicious. That story could have been true, and angry husbands can make a mess of a guy. But there was no one else in the shop.

The hairdresser picked up the receipt and came round the front of the shop. Hicky had an idea for a moment the guy was going to lay hands on him, but that was only his over-suspicious brain at work imagining things. The hairdresser went to the door and looked carefully at the receipt.

Then he turned and came back into the shop. Hicky was looking beyond him, to see if that manoeuvre had been a signal to anyone outside, but no one was approaching.

'We've got to be careful.' That was the hairdresser speaking. 'We get into trouble with our customers if we part with their letters to anyone.' He was rifling through some letters in a drawer behind the counter. Came up with one. It felt very thin to Hicky. There couldn't have been much love and affection inside that envelope; there wasn't room for it.

Hicky took the letter and walked to the door. He felt that the hairdresser was watching him. Hicky was suddenly uneasy. Everything was working out too easily; there was a catch in it, because guys don't get on to five hundred and fifty bucks so easily.

He looked on to the busy sidewalk, but no one was looking his way. Suddenly he ducked out and went hurrying towards the El.

Fifty yards down the street a car came alongside him, and a man leaned out holding a short stick in his hands. The stick started to smoke and make a noise faintly heard above the roar of the El, and a licking little flame kept spitting from the end of it.

Then the car drove off.

Some people vaguely thought there was something wrong. Maybe there was a bit more noise than usual. Or it might have been instinct that told them. But no one screamed, no one shouted. Not yet for a minute.

And in that minute Hicky died. He was on his knees as the car drove off. His bright, brown, mousy eyes were looking down at his hands, clasped to his middle, and there was surprise in them, because there was blood on his fingers. His blood. And it was very bright.

He was still watching when, seconds later, his eyes suddenly glazed in death and he crumpled forward on to his face. His legs looked very thin and skinny, sticking out from under his pants.

2

Girl on a plane

They brought Cheyenne Charlie on to the case, which shows that suddenly it ranked as important. For Charlie, real name Charlie Chey . . . held the rank of inspector in the F.B.I. and was a special operator, assigned only to the most difficult cases. And, incidentally, the most dangerous.

He came up the steps that led into the Skymaster, and there was the taste of blood in his mouth. At the top he looked round at the Los Angeles airport from which he was departing for New York. He didn't like leaving the warm, sunny Pacific coast for New York's baking, summer heat, fouled with the stink of half a million auto exhausts. But they'd sent for him; told him to catch the first plane out. There was something big cooking in N.Y.

He ducked and went inside the shadowy interior of the plane. It was roasting hot there, because the Skymaster had been standing out on the concrete apron in the sun too long and was like a glasshouse. Even the nyloned queen who was their hostess was running rivulets down the careful make-up on her face. She was trying to get people quickly settled in their seats, and was anxious to be taking off because then it would be cooler, even pleasantly cool, up in the cloudless Californian sky.

Cheyenne Charlie hefted his bulk between the rows of seats and sat down against an emergency door. He was a careful man, Cheyenne Charlie. He always sat next to an emergency exit when he was flying. He was a bold, resolute man, but he didn't go in for bravado or take unnecessary risks, which is why he was an F.B.I. special operator.

He accepted all the arguments about the high safety factor attached to modern civil aviation, but he went right on sitting next to an emergency door because statistics also proved that crashes do happen, and when they do the fellow next to a door has a slightly better chance of getting clear than the other passengers.

A girl came down between the seats, looked round, saw him, went on and then came back and sat next to him. The light was on saying. 'No Smoking, Fasten Safety Belts.' The girl had hers fastened before Cheyenne had worked out what type this airline used. He didn't look at the girl. He had a theory that if he looked at a girl he lost her.

Then he remembered that the girl had looked at him, had seen that battered face of his, and then had come back to this seat next to him.

Cheyenne, seventy-four inches tall without his crépe-soled footwear, two hundred pounds registering every time he got on to a weighing machine, had no illusions about his appearance. He had had to work his way through college, and the work he had chosen had done things to his face. But it had paid well. He thought it had been worth it all . . . the fists that had pounded his ears flat, the oak-hard elbows that had altered the contours of his big, good-humoured face.

All-in wrestling leaves its mark on a man.

But it had paid for his studies, and enabled him to major in law. And when he went with his bright new degree to the F.B.I. he had found his brawn no drawback, though the F.B.I. always picked their men for brain first.

He had found another factor of assistance in his work. His blood. He was one of the few full-blooded Indians in the Bureau, and his Spartan early life in the reservation, where he had learned to track and hunt and acquire stamina from hard trails, had been of infinite value to him many times when manhunting.

And that blood was in his mouth now. He settled back in his seat as the plane lurched across to the end of the runway, and his tongue explored a hole in the top of his mouth. A boot had applied the dentistry to that late-lamented tooth.

The boot had belonged to a man. He was a Hollywood heel. A man in love with his profile, but nobody else thought much of it. So a fellow has to live, and when he couldn't get work mugging before a camera, he had set up a nice blackmail racket with some other rats.

When one victim couldn't stand it and ate a bagful of sleeping tablets, the F.B.I. came in. Cheyenne Charlie (he'd taken the name of Charlie Chey when he came off the reservation, so everybody promptly switched things around a little and called him Cheyenne Charlie) after a couple of weeks trapped one of the rats.

There had been some welcome resistance, and Cheyenne had avenged the blackmailed victims with some mighty cruel treatment. All the same, the rat had got his foot into Cheyenne's mouth once . . .

The girl next to him said, 'You're a cop aren't you? A G-man?'

The plane was starting away. Charlie turned and looked at her. She was a pert, attractive creature, as nice as any that ever took a fellow home to meet mom. Hair that was blonde, but not too much so and had dark strands running through the waves. Eyes that were blue and quick with intelligence. A bright gal, he thought.

'What gives you that idea?' He was looking at her thoughtfully. People didn't deliberately sit next to a G-man unless they had things on their mind.

'Twice before I've seen you. Once you came in from Indiana with one of the Oakland gang. Remember? Another time the handcuffs were on a guy who'd done things with an ice pick, so the Los Angeles papers told me next day.'

'So?'

'So maybe you can help me.' The girl sat half round in her seat. They took off at that moment, but neither noticed they were airborne.

Cheyenne sighed. 'You don't need to tell me any more. You want to be a G-girl. All the girls I meet do. They think it's like on the movies, with plenty of fun and wisecrackin' and everything nicely tied up with a wedding ring after ninety minutes.'

He reflected. 'Now, I'd guess you're an air-hostess. Most girls think that's the most glamorous job in the world. Why don't you stay at it?' The slick, practised way she'd fastened her seat belt had given him the idea she was a hostess.

She tossed her head. 'Glamour? We're only glorified waitresses, handing cups of coffee round. Only, we don't get tips. Anyway, I'm an ex-hostess.'

'Fired?'

'Fired,' said the girl, nodding. She brooded over the indignity.

'One of our vice-presidents tried to get fresh. I hit him with the first thing handy ... some tomato ketchup. And his wife was back with the passengers.'

'So he fired you?'

'On the spot.'

'And now they're shipping you home in disgrace. What's your name?' This girl tickled his sense of humour. There was something refreshing about her directness, her candour.

She paused, then delivered herself. 'It's October. October Raine.'

Cheyenne said, 'My God, I'll never believe that! October's a name they give to cold wet months and to revolutions in Tsarist Russia. But it's not a girl's name.' Accusingly. 'Honey, you gave yourself that name!'

She pouted, then admitted reluctantly,

'Well, maybe I did. But it's a nice name, and that's the only one you'll get from me.' Her hand touched his sleeve earnestly. 'Mister, if you knew what a plain name I've really got, you wouldn't blame me.'

Cheyenne's eyes twinkled. 'Then, October, I'll never ask you for it. And come to think of it, October's a right smart, attractive name. Someday when I get me a family of G-kids I'll try'n remember it.'

October asked, softly, 'So . . . you'll help me become a G-girl, huh?'

The air-hostess came up with an armful of newspapers. Cheyenne helped himself to a new-flown in *New York Herald*. He opened it as he said, 'There isn't a thing I c'n do for you, October. The Bureau don't employ G-girls. Sometimes if they have special need for a woman on a case, they go out and get one temporarily.'

Her face was falling. He patted her hand. 'Go to another airline and get yourself a job as hostess,' he advised kindly. 'Make sure they haven't too many vice-presidents and I guess you'll get along all right.'

He opened the paper. There were pictures, headlines. The words *Street Assassination* leapt out of the page. He skimmed the story quickly, looked closely at the photograph of the murdered man. He didn't recognise him.

He put the paper down and wondered what important case it could be that he was being put on. He didn't think it could be the street assassination case, because that simple murder . . . wasn't seemingly sufficient to warrant bringing a special operator right across the American continent to tackle it.

The girl didn't mention a job with the Bureau after that. Cheyenne's answer had been too authoritative to permit argument. And they talked of everything but crime during that long night and morning flight across to the Atlantic seaboard.

* * *

They were glad to see Cheyenne so soon in the big New York offices of the Bureau. He was taken right in to see the chief without any delay. The chief had a paper spread on his desk before him. Cheyenne saw that the Street Assassination had prominent place in it. And he thought: So my case has something to do with that murder.

The chief said, 'You've been brought here, Chey, because you're not well known this side of America We're up against something big, and maybe it's as well for us to make a new start on the case and have a fresh mind to direct things. Now you know why you were dragged off a case in L.A.'

Then he got down to telling the story . . . told of the Blond Boys and the car that disappeared in well-lighted streets with everyone watching for it, and the pirate transmitter that was making a fool of the New York police and now of the F.B.I.

The first record they had of the Blond Boys was one night when an alert watchman spotted furs being taken from a warehouse. They got away with some, but because the watchman tripped off the shattering police alarm, they fled and left most of their intended haul behind.

He had been near enough to see the gang at work, and he reported something curious. Not a man wore a hat. Every man was a blond. 'An' they were so much alike, dang me if they mightn't ha' bin brothers,' was his statement. No one took much heed of that, because night watchmen become colourful in their accounts after robberies.

What happened immediately the Blond Boys got into their cars (they were using two big sedans) was much more interesting.

In the first place, quite a lot of people saw those cars, and all were agreed that they were vivid yellow, like New York cabs. Those vivid yellow cars careered out on to a long, busy, well-lit street with no side turnings to it. A lot of people saw them enter that street. But no one, including several cops, remembered seeing any yellow cars pass at the time the mobsters were escaping.

They got away, then, those crooks, but very cleverly they made sure of escaping by immobilising for ten minutes the entire police force of New York.

Cheyenne, listening to the story, looked startled at that. 'This didn't get into the papers?'

'We suppressed it. We don't want the public to be alarmed by this gang's activities.' And then the chief explained what he meant by his dramatic statement.

Immediately the watchman started the alarm bells shrilling, a radio transmitter went on the air . . . a pirate station. It operated on the frequency employed by the police, and for ten minutes it jammed every attempt on the part of the police radio operators to send out a warning to their radio patrol cars. So, because they hadn't been warned, police sat in their cars while the criminals escaped.

Cheyenne said, 'There are a lot of things to puzzle out in this case, chief.' He was thinking of all-alike blonds, cars that dissolved in thin air, and pirate transmitters that could paralyse a police system based upon radio communication.

The chief said, 'We think the Blond Boys have pulled off several good hauls without being detected, and so without needing to resort to their pirate transmitter. But they've used it again since.'

The second time was also at night. It was a robbery of gold bullion. That was very recent. A passing patrolman got suspicious of a big yellow car and raised the alarm. He, too, reported seeing a gang of seven blond men escaping with the gold; he and a lot of other people saw that yellow car race out on to a busy, well-lighted thoroughfare. But nobody remembered seeing a yellow car after that.

And the police weren't interested anyway, because HQ didn't tell them to watch out for a yellow car containing seven blond men. Because HQ couldn't . . . that pirate transmitter was effectually jamming any attempt to transmit messages to mobile units of the police.

Suddenly, close on midnight not much more than a week ago, every radio car in New York had been alerted by a message that ordered every car in Hoboken to go at once to the Hoboken Land Bank, where a robbery was in progress.

'That message didn't come from any

police transmitter,' said the chief. 'We think it came from the pirate transmitter. We think the operator of the transmitter tried to double-cross the gang and get them trapped. But he failed. Maybe the gang was tuned in to the police wavelength just as a precaution. The moment they heard that warning they got outa the place ahead of the cops.

'They were seen, of course, and everything followed as before except for one thing. They were blond men seen running to two big, yellow cars. The cars ran out among other traffic . . . and disappeared.'

'And the transmitter?'

'For once this time after warning the police it didn't try to hamper them by any jamming tactics. Even so, we never found any yellow cars, containing seven blond boys. They got away.'

Cheyenne said, 'You're reading about the Street Assassination crime. Does that fit into this Blond Boys' set up?'

The chief nodded. 'Somehow it does. We don't quite see where, but . . . A fellar named Hickman Gue — a no-good little guy who's acted as stoolpigeon to the police in between spells for petty larceny, blackmail and more sordid offences . . . collected a letter from an accommodation address and was mown down by machinegun fire when he stepped out on to the sidewalk.

'How do we know it was the Blond Boys' did it? Because the moment they opened up, so did that pirate transmitter, with the result that the car got clean away without being detected.'

Cheyenne asked, 'That car . . . it wasn't yellow was it?'

The chief said, 'Not this time. It was a black sedan.'

'So they use yellow cars by night, but black cars by day.'

The chief looked at him sharply, wondering if there was anything behind that remark. Then Cheyenne said, 'They must have found a new operator for their transmitter. Maybe it was a revenge act. Maybe Gue was the double-crossing operator, so they liquidated him.'

The chief said, 'Maybe. Only Gue didn't know the first thing about radio, and had just come outa stir. So . . . guess again, brother, guess again.'

Cheyenne's mind was racing. He guessed, 'There was nothing in that envelope when it was opened . . . that letter, I mean, that little Gue collected from the hairdresser.'

The chief lifted his eyebrows. 'Right first time. It was empty, and there were no fingerprints on it. It was simply addressed to 'Jay Gee' at that accommodation address.'

'The hairdresser's story?'

'He says a fat guy came in and made arrangements to have mail left there. Didn't leave a forwarding address but said he'd collect periodically. But he never came back. Instead a couple of guys came in . . . dark fellars both, but the hairdresser doesn't give much description of them. They said they'd a blackmailing letter from Jay Gee, said they didn't want to go to the cops about it until they knew who the guy was sending 'em letters.

'Well, it seemed a good story, and when they came across with five bucks the hairdresser was willing to tip them off when anyone came to collect the letter. He was to come to the door and wave a piece of paper . . . in his case it was the collector's receipt . . . so's the men would know Jay Gee or a friend of his had called.'

'And that's all the fellar knows about the crime?'

'That's all.' The chief rose. 'But I reckon you'd better get down and see that hairdresser. He seems the only guy we know who's been at close quarters with the Blond Boys.'

Cheyenne was on his feet. 'You said the pair that came to see the hairdresser were dark, both of 'em?'

'Sure.' The chief's face wore that expression of resigned perplexity. 'But the boy with the typewriter and his two companions waiting out there in the car for Hicky Gue were both blonds. The hairdresser didn't see them, but a lot of people did.'

Cheyenne nodded, and it seemed to the chief that there was just the slightest trace of satisfaction about the special operator.

He said, suspiciously, 'You wouldn't have got on to anything, would you? Not already?'

But when next he looked, Cheyenne's rugged bronze face was impassive. 'Not yet, chief. But . . . let's hope it won't be long before I do. Guess I'll go down town and start that trail from the hairdresser's.'

He went down to the street level. At the long desk with its confidential grilles like in a bank, he saw a figure that was familiar.

He hoped he hadn't been seen and went swiftly out through a side entrance. At once the stifling heat of a New York summer hit up at him, and promptly his thoughts turned to a place where all drinks were long and cool.

The place was where he remembered it. Outside he bought an afternoon edition, then went inside through the revolving doors. Inside was as cool as Boston in early May. He climbed on to a tall stool, feeling suddenly refreshed, and waited for a barman.

While waiting he opened the paper to the page with the latest details about the street assassination crime. He was reading when the barman came up, so he folded the paper at the place he'd got to and slipped it into his suit coat pocket.

He said, 'Make it long, make it cold, and if it's got beer in it, it'll be just right.'

Someone behind him said, 'And you can put my name to that order, too, brother.'

Cheyenne sighed. 'Even though it's a name she cooked up for herself,' he told the barman, and then he turned and looked at October Raine. She was smiling. She looked good. Summer heat and a long night in a plane hadn't seemed to touch her.

Cheyenne said, 'I'm too tired to work it out, so you tell me. Start with your visit to the Appointments desk, back there.' His head jerked roughly in the direction of the F.B.I. building.

She stripped off some perfectly useless fishnet gloves. She wasn't a bit nonplussed or bothered. 'I got me a job with the F.B.I.'

'As a G-girl?' Cheyenne was grinning because he knew she hadn't.

'As a stenog.' She put her elbows on the bar, clasped her fingers together and delicately balanced her pointed chin on them. She was very cool, very poised. Then she gave him a winning smile.

Two beers came up in tall glasses. Cheyenne paid for both. Politely he enquired, 'And can you . . . stenog? Or is it like October . . . something you thought up?'

She said, sweetly, 'I am a very good stenog. I can take shorthand so fast you'd be amazed, and my typing is really hot.' He looked at her slim fingers and thought that perhaps she wasn't exaggerating.

So he asked, 'And why did you decide to go back to stenogging . . . and start with the F.B.I.?'

She stopped posing then and became a pleading girl. 'Oh, look, Charles, do try to help a girl. You said that when the F.B.I. have need for a girl on a case they co-opt one temporarily. Well, Charles, why shouldn't it be me, an F.B.I. employee? And if you knew of my existence, wouldn't it be so easy for you to ask for me?'

Cheyenne said, 'It would.' He drank. 'But I'm not likely to need a girl assistant.' He drank again. 'And I don't remember telling you my name was Charles.'

She said, 'I got it from the flight manifest list before we left the plane.'

Cheyenne sighed. This girl sure was a go-getter. A smart kid.

So he said, 'You're good. Okay, you tell me where I'm going now and maybe I will remember your name if we needed a G-girl.'

Promptly she answered, 'You're going down to see the hairdresser mentioned in that Street Assassination case.'

3

Deadpan

Cheyenne called for two tall encores to the first beers. The girl by his side waited for him to speak, and he knew that she was tense and watchful, trying to interpret every little movement of his . . . trying even to understand his silence.

So he kept her waiting. He found he was enjoying this second, unexpected meeting. This girl was stimulating company.

The drinks came and he drank half his glass immediately. The girl left hers untouched. Then Cheyenne spoke, gently.

'Honey, you're a great guesser. And that's all it was, an inspired guess. It could so easily have been wrong, miles wrong. You hadn't a clue, until your eyes saw the Street Assassination headline in this newspaper I just bought. We'd read about the case, flyin' down, so you remembered the hairdresser guy and added him to your guess.' He sighed. 'Admit it, October Raine, it was a lucky guess, wasn't it?'

She nodded meekly, her eyes downcast. So he patted her hand and said, 'Guess you'll be a right smart stenog for one of the desk brigade. If ever I need one, I'll send for you.'

He finished his glass, then got down from the stool. He felt better now.

October said, in a small voice, 'I don't start till next week. I've got nothing to do, Mr. Chey. Can't I go with you and see how a G-man operates?'

Cheyenne grinned to himself. The minx was doing everything to get along with him, even to calling him Mr. Chey now. But it was no good.

'We don't work well with an audience,' he said pleasantly, and just as pleasantly he promised, 'If I catch you following me I'll give you over to a nice big Irish cop to look after.'

And she knew he meant it and would do it without hesitation. He went out, leaving her looking mournful over a long, cooling drink.

The cigar-store-cum-hairdresser's depressed him. All this section of New York, crowded, stinking vaguely of cabbage water and gasoline fumes, raised in him a longing for the lovely Pacific coast he had just left. New York . . . downtown New York, especially . . . was no place to be in early summer.

He stood inside the shop and looked at the glass cases with their cigars and impressive-sealed cigar boxes. It was shabby and dingy and altogether unprepossessing. A bell had rung somewhere in the back as he stepped on to the mat, crossing the threshold. Within seconds the glass-panelled door opened and a thin, lined-faced, grey-headed man wearing steel-rimmed glasses came through. He was wearing a white, knee-length coat, and was stuffing comb and scissors into a monogrammed breast pocket.

When he saw Cheyenne he dropped the false smile he had been wearing, and instead said, sourly, 'Betcha you don't buy much, mister. Betcha you're a cop or a noospaper man.'

Cheyenne was always willing to learn.

He said, good-humouredly, 'You tell me how you know I'm no customer.'

The hairdresser took off his glasses and wiped the weariness out of his eyes with the back of his hands.

'Funny thing I've noticed about customers. They don't ever stand with both hands stuck deep in their pockets. They're either fiddlin' around for money or just standing with their hands outa their pockets. But not standing like you with hands shoved down right to the bottom of the linings. Cops always stand like that.'

Cheyenne said, 'You've got the makings of a cop yourself, brother.' But the way the fellar looked, he didn't take it as a compliment. Cheyenne thought that in this neighbourhood maybe cops weren't considered respectable.

So Cheyenne delicately glossed over the silence by producing his identification shield in its leather case. The hairdresser said, 'F.B.I.,' and stopped looking quite so apathetic.

But he hadn't much to tell beyond what the chief had already told him. His description of the two men who had

44

slipped him five bucks wasn't detailed.

'They were a coupla Italians,' he kept saying vaguely. 'Blue chins an' sideboards an' plenty eye, if you know what I mean.' Cheyenne nodded. 'When the cops took me for questioning, they showed me a pile of photographs so high, but it didn't help. After a while I could have sworn half of 'em had been the guys that had come here that day.'

'You saw the Blond Boys in their car?'

'Yeah. I was kinda interested, so when the li'l guy went out with Jay Gee's letter I stood at the door to watch after him. There was a car parked down the street a bit. I remembered seeing it there earlier, though I didn't think it was waitin' for anyone in particular. You know what I mean, cars are always parkin' up for as long as the cops'll let 'em; we get a lot of 'em.'

'What happened?' Cheyenne's question put the hairdresser back on the story.

'I didn't see at first. There was a big truck parked outside. I saw the li'l fellar seem to go down on his knees an' pray a bit, and then collapse altogether on to the sidewalk. I didn't hear anything because of the El. Then I realised something was seriously wrong, an' I looked quickly into the street an' saw a car drivin' away just beyond the big truck. I also saw a tommy gun barrel as it was pulled back into the sedan.'

'And you saw the occupants of the car?'

They had to wait for a moment before the hairdresser could answer; the shop shook and seemed to fill with the roar of agonised steel from the overhead Elevated.

The hairdresser said, 'You see why nobody heard that tommy much. Nobody hears anythin' when that thing goes by. But you get used to it in time.'

'The men?' Cheyenne steered him back again.

'I didn't catch more'n a glimpse of 'em. You'll find other people saw 'em better . . . the cops have their names. They were fair haired, not like the fellars that came to see me.' He wrinkled his nose thoughtfully. Someone shouted in the back. 'Somehow they all kinda looked alike. Deadpan, with flat, blond curls.

They looked . . . ' He was struggling for words. 'Looked kinda dead themselves.'

Cheyenne was listening intently. When he felt there was nothing more to learn about the men he asked, 'What did you notice about the car?'

The hairdresser looked out at the patch of sunlight. His thoughts were far away. Again someone shouted from the back room, but the hairdresser didn't seem to hear it. Cheyenne waited patiently, because he knew that what the hairdresser was thinking had some bearing on the question he had asked.

The man sighed and took off his spectacles and rubbed them on some tissue paper. A growing roar from the El stopped his reply for the moment. When the clatter had died into the distance, the hairdresser said, 'It's got me to thinkin', what I said about them guys in the car. About 'em lookin' dead.'

Cheyenne prompted, 'Why?'

The hairdresser looked uncertainly at him and then replied, 'Because I just remembered that car looked kinda dead, too.'

He blinked behind his glasses. 'Don't get me wrong, mister. It's just a thought came to me. It's funny how you start to remember things a long time afterwards, an' what I've just told you I didn't even remember to tell the cops. But that car did look dead. It was big and a new model, a Packard, someone else said. But it didn't have the glossy finish that every car has nowadays. It was . . . well, kinda dull, kinda dead lookin'.'

He looked anxiously at Cheyenne. 'You don't think me screwy?'

Cheyenne said, 'No. It's little things that sometimes grow to be important. Like dead pans an' dead autos. I won't forget it.'

He was about to go when the back door leading to the hairdressing saloon jerked open. A man came into the shop. He was wearing a white smock round his front and his hair was messed up. He glared at the hairdresser, then snatched the smock from his neck and hurled it to the ground.

'The hell,' he said peevishly. 'You think I'm gonna stay back there all day while you make mouth noises with your playmates? The hell,' he snapped indignantly and stamped out.

The hairdresser groaned. 'I clean forgot him. Look, G-man, I gotta get back. There's another guy in their readin' funnies. Maybe he'll get tired an' walk out soon, too. If there's nothin' more . . . ?'

Cheyenne shook his head. There wasn't anything else he could think of. So the hairdresser bolted back into the rear room, and Cheyenne went out into the hot sunlight again.

He stood there irresolute, trying to picture the scene, and getting some idea of it. Then he walked towards the El until he came to the scene of the killing . . . fifty yards from the hairdresser's, the chief had said. It didn't look unlike any other piece of sidewalk, and it told him just . . . nothing.

It was while he was looking abstractedly down at the litter in the gutter that he began to hear shouting as the roaring el passed into the distance. Then he saw people running.

So he started to run himself, back the

way he had just come.

He pounded up, the heat forgotten, his brown face grim because he knew there'd been another serious happening . . .

When he was through the little crowd at the entrance to the hairdresser's he saw the grey-haired man. He had lost his glasses, and there was blood down his face. Two men were supporting him. Blood was pouring on to their hands from a mess where his nose had been. But he knew Cheyenne when he came up.

'What happened?' the G-man rapped.

They lowered the hairdresser to the floor and let him lean against the glass-fronted counter. He was game; he tried all he could to tell Cheyenne what had happened.

'It was that guy sittin' back waitin' for me. Guess he could ha' heard everything by the door.' That damned el again. They had to wait till it died down. A cop came shoving through the crowd and began to make a noise. Cheyenne turned and snarled at him, and the patrolman must have thought he was a doctor and at once quit beefing.

'He just said, 'Brother, you open that yap too much. You got too good a memory.' Then he smacked me in the face with the butt of a gun. He kept on doin' it . . . ' They had to wait while the hairdresser fought to get breath. 'When I fell to the floor he kicked me a few times. Then he said, 'If we find you opening your yap to cops again, brother, I'll be back to see you.' Then he went.'

He had guts; he went right on talking, though his voice was now down to a whisper.

Cheyenne said, 'What was the fellar like?'

The crowd parted to let men with a stretcher come through. But Cheyenne wouldn't allow them to lift the hairdresser yet. This man might hold the clue to set him off on the trail; he had to get it out of him without delay, if it were there.

The bleeding, half-conscious man fought for memory. 'He was big . . . blond guy.'

'Blond?' repeated Cheyenne softly. Blonds figured a lot in New York crime right now.

There was an expression of puzzlement

on the victim's face . . . or it might only have been in those pain-narrowed eyes. There was something he couldn't understand, and it seemed to be worrying him.

'I don't get it. He was blond, but I don't remember leavin' no blond in that room when I came to speak to you. But maybe I didn't see well because he sat with his back to the light.' That el roaring up from the distance, thundering overhead, then mercifully fading.

When it was gone Cheyenne prompted urgently, because the hairdresser was fast slipping into unconsciousness . . . the interns with the stretcher-bearers were getting impatient; someone in the crowd raised a yowl that they were letting the poor guy bleed to death.

'That blond guy . . . something's on your mind, brother. What is it? What's puzzling you?'

The hairdresser stirred, got words out again, but so slowly now. 'Didn't move his mouth when he talked . . . face like putty . . . a deadpan if ever I've seen one . . . that's it, a real deadpan.' The thought seemed to bring on a mild excitement and he tried to lift himself. His eyes were wider now than they'd been all during the questioning. Almost horrified he began to shout, 'It was a dead guy done it . . . a guy with a dead face . . . the father'n mother of all deadpans . . . '

And then he lost consciousness and the interns took over. One of them said, 'The guy went hysterical. It's sight of their own blood does it. Now, me, I don't get affected at all.'

He was young, brash, a show-off. Cheyenne said, 'Look well after him, Dracula. That guy did well to tell me all that after the threat the deadpan gave him.'

And then he went to the office to consider all that he had learned. One thing he was certain of. That observant hairdresser hadn't been indulging in hysteria when he'd talked of a dead face. There was something behind it all, behind this talk of deadpans and . . . dead-looking cars. But for the life in him Cheyenne couldn't figure out what, yet.

★   ★   ★

Little more than a hundred miles away was a girl who was soon to see a man without a face. She was unconscious, inside a sedan which was ingeniously fitted so that nitrous oxide ... an anaesthetic better known as Laughing Gas ... could be injected in upon the passenger or passengers by turning a valve alongside the seat of the driver.

The driver was a quivering jelly of fear. He had strong hands, but the rest of him was soft.

It was Joe Gell.

4

The tortured girl

Joe Gell sat in a big chair that felt damp, as all the house felt damp, even though it was summer and outside the sun was shining strongly. There was a dank smell everywhere, the smell you get when you open up a house after it has been without occupants for a long time.

He slumped there, a huddle of suit and man, his eyes blinking nervously behind thick-lensed glasses. On the carpet before him, stirring in a pool of sunshine from the window, was a slim-limbed girl, a blonde.

Vaguely he remembered that he had an oxygen cylinder somewhere in the house, and that would bring her round quickly, but cylinders are weighty things and Joe Gell's strength didn't go past his wrists. That was why the girl was on the floor and not on the broad, comfortable divan.

Joe had dragged her so far, but hadn't found the strength or the will to lift her into a more comfortable place. He hadn't much strength at all, and he hadn't any guts, this formless man called Joe Gell, though he could do a lot of curiously daring things, like many a gutless man.

Like kidnapping this girl. Phoning in a false voice and telling her he had a message for her . . . she had to get ready at once and come to town in a car that would come and pick her up. And the name he had used was one that few men would have dared take in vain

And then he'd waited, made up, of course, dying a thousand deaths, because if she had had a momentary suspicion, if she had recognised his voice and rung through to that number that wasn't in the book, it would have meant some tight-lipped guys suddenly coming out of the block towards his car and not this girl. They'd have had modern lethal methods of despatch in their hands, and they would have used them, too.

They might even have been blond and deadpan but that wouldn't have been for his benefit but in case passersby saw anything happen.

He found himself thinking it was queer, he'd invented deadpan, and now it was a potential weapon against him.

But the girl hadn't suspected. She had come down the steps and straight across to the car. She had been annoyed about something, and her voice had snapped as she got inside, speaking to the driver all the time. And she hadn't recognised him.

He'd started the car, then twiddled the valve. He'd heard her talking over the hand mike, and then whatever she was saying . . . he wasn't listening to her words . . . got slower and slower and then finally she was quiet. He looked round then and saw she was lolling as if drunk on the seat. As they went round a corner she slid down into the space between the seats and seemed to crouch there. He didn't stop and attempt to move her into a more comfortable position. She was safer there, out of sight.

He drove without stopping until he came to this house he had once used, back in his early days in New York, before going out to Los Angeles. It was in a remote place in the Catskills, not in the fashionable holiday part but still in a pretty lovely place.

As he sat there and waited for the girl to recover, he could look out over a sea of trees, mostly pines so high up. There was also a glimpse of water through the branches in several places, where the big reservoirs that served New York lay.

It was a lovely scene, as lovely as anything to be found in the wide American continent, but Joe Gell didn't look at it. He was looking at the girl. To him she was lovelier than any mountain scenery.

Then she began to move more strongly and to groan as though coming out of a hangover. Joe sat, his eyes blinking as if nervously awaiting the opening of her eyes.

She opened them. They were baby blue. She looked up at the ceiling, dancing with reflected lights, turned and looked at the sun-bright window, then quickly shut her eyes against the light. Then she sat up, holding her head, shook it gently and then opened her eyes again and saw Joe Gell.

At once the lipstick smeared mouth opened and showed lipstick stained teeth and she cried out with fright. And being unoriginal she said the obvious thing, 'You!'

Joe seemed to get agitated and fidgeted around in the chair and clasped his big hands and then unclasped them, and he looked so babyish and tremulous that it was impossible to think that he could cook up the nicest schemes for killing people . . . people he had never met, people who had done him no harm.

The girl shrilled, 'What's happened? Where am I? What are you doing with me?' And her small, oval face showed fear as she looked round at the unfamiliar room.

He didn't answer. Just sat gaping. His white, unwholesomeness giving him the appearance of a soft fat grub, and the way his myopic staring kept his head weaving in constant motion heightened the illusion.

The girl lost her fear. He was too

contemptible for anyone to be afraid of him. She got to her feet, and her voice came up shrill and indignant. She was beginning to understand her position now, and she didn't express herself nicely.

'Jeez, you'll pay for this. And how you'll pay! When Maurice hears of this he'll finish you . . . he said he would when he got that letter!'

Joe Gell quivered at her words. He begged, 'Don't talk like that. I can't stand pain, you know I can't. And just talking about it makes me feel bad, very bad. Pet, I want you to start liking me. Pet, you've got to like me; there's nothing else I want in the world but that. I've lived for you and loved you ever since that day I saw you on the set in Hollywood. I've never loved anyone like you.'

His voice sounded weak, almost as though he were going to cry. The girl had pulled herself up on to the settee. Something bright on her ankle attracted her attention; she had a feeling that something encircled her knee. But his maudlin confession diverted her attention again.

She fluffed her hair and started to tidy herself, while she got nasty with him.

'That's why you followed when I came to New York . . . to Maurice. I thought it was just chance, meeting you. An' I guess that's why you were so ready to join Maurice's crowd . . . to be near me, huh?'

It was the first time in her cheap life that Pet Deganya hadn't felt flattered because of a man's attentions. But then Joe Gell wasn't a man. He was an unhealthy crawling slug, and no girl could feel for a hunk of dead flesh like that. Just to think of it made a cold wave travel down her spine, and then a second followed when she realised that he had kidnapped her and she had been unconscious for quite some time . . .

She jumped to her feet, her voice shrilling again. 'I'm gettin' outa here. You lowdown swab, you got no right to treat me like this.' Under stress Pet Deganya forgot the elocution she had learned at Hollywood and instead returned to the argot of her childhood in the Polish section of Detroit, where language can be eloquent, to the point, but highly crude.

She started to rush to the door, and Joe Gell didn't say anything. At the door she stopped. Her right leg was stuck out into the air behind her. She gasped, then turned on her left leg.

A steel-bright bracelet encircled her right ankle; another her knee. An insulated wire ran from the foot of a very heavy workbench and connected with the bracelets.

Joe Gell . . . she thought how appropriate was the name Maurice's boys had contemptuously given him, Jelly Joe . . . heaved himself out of the deep chair and went across to the bench. There was a small switchboard back of it, and Joe put out his hand to a switch.

His voice had changed when he spoke. There was a kind of distant regret in it.

'You think me a fool, Pet. Everyone thinks I'm a fool. But I'm not, you've all seen I'm not. I can look ahead and anticipate. I knew you would try to walk out on me when you came to, so I fixed you to this little instrument.' She saw something swinging, like a pendulum on a clock, or a metronome on a piano.

He sighed and said, 'I guessed, too, you would . . . spurn me. So I fixed things to cover that, too. You'll never cut your way through that anklet or through the cable. And I can do things with those two electrodes attached to your leg.'

A chill of horror gripped her then, because she was remembering all the clever things this man could do.

His voice went higher, and there was a thin, ragged edge to the sound so that it was akin to hysteria.

'But you spurned me! You insulted me! You didn't have any consideration for my feelings. You never have had. You and all your friends. You have gone out of your way to insult me, to hurt me, to say things that lashed me and left me feeling bad and burning up inside. Oh, yes, you did all this. Yet I went on loving you, and I thought if only I could tell you of my love you would be different.'

Suddenly in his rage he beat upon the bench with those big work-calloused hands of his, and a little froth appeared on his lips as he stormed at her. 'And you only insulted me. You called me names.

63

You threw my love back at me.'

And with that he flicked down the switch and watched the effect it had on her.

She screamed, and with a sudden, convulsive leap crashed unconscious on to the floor before the settee.

5

Man without a face

Joe Gell sat on the plain, hard chair against the bench, his hand still on the switch, his eyes looking broodingly through his thick lenses at the limp figure on the floor. Then the girl moaned and stirred and rolled so that her tear-stained, red-smeared face was towards him. Her hair was an untidy mess, and her opening eyes looked through it with something of the furtiveness and fear of a defenceless animal.

If Joe Gell had looked closer he would have seen that under the lipstick her lips were slightly blue, and as she struggled into a sitting position her hand pressed against her side.

She moaned into words, begging for compassion. 'Joe, don't hurt me agen! Don't do it, Joe. God, that hurt, that did! Why did you have to do it? I'll do anything for you, anything . . . only don't do that agen.' And she wept.

Joe Gell stirred and spoke. His voice seemed thinner than normal, even more high-pitched and child-like. And his manner varied between weak, bullying attack, and nervous, uncertain defence for what he had done.

His voice trembled as he answered, 'You gave me hell often enough, Pet. You and your smart cracks and sneers. You thought I didn't mind, and if I did mind, the hell, so what? I was Jelly Joe, the slob, the crawler, the slug. The thing to be laughed at, to be shoved around and given the worst of everything . . . the lousiest place to sleep, the food that no one else would touch. Oh, Jelly Joe won't mind . . . that was it always! Joe's too dumb to feel and to understand!

'Well, I did feel!' His voice went up again. 'All the time I was burnin' up inside, all the time I was hatin' it, and hatin' everybody. All the time I wanted to kill people, to get my hands on them and make them suffer. And that's what I'm goin' to do!'

He was thumping on the bench with his big, hard hands, a big fat, babyish man on the borders of hysteria again. Pet Deganya was scared, terrified. And her voice wailed, 'But why do you have to do it me, Joe? You said yourself you loved me. Why d'you want to hurt me, honey?'

'But you don't love me, Pet,' Joe Gell said pathetically. 'You never will, either. You'll string me along now with a lot of words that don't mean anything, and when you get a chance you'll just run out on me, won't you? Only, I'm not going to let you get away with it. You'll pay for all you've made me suffer while I was with you.'

Pet whispered, her eyes on him, 'We didn't know you were suffering, Joe. You never said anything. If I'd have known, I wouldn't have let them, honest I wouldn't. They just thought it was fun, that was all.'

Joe said, 'It wasn't fun, none of it.' And his eyes were blinking quickly behind his glasses, remembering. 'It was hell. But . . . you know what was the worst part?'

She shook her dumb blonde head,

wondering. The tears had dried on her cheeks, and they felt stiff and taut.

'It was being there, living there . . . and knowing you belonged to Maurice.'

And suddenly he slipped his fat carcase off the chair and started to walk slowly towards her, and his pale face was whiter now than ever. He was indulging in a bath of emotional self-sympathy, a neurotic nearly round the bend at that moment, had Pet Deganya known it.

He was getting nearer, and the girl was in terror again. And then she heard . . . just a sound. Outside.

Her eyes swung to the window. But there was nothing, no one there.

And yet she was convinced that there was someone lurking just outside the window.

Desperately she battled for time. For if there was someone outside, they must surely help her or get help to her.

She crept away to the full extent of the line, then started talking. She talked quickly, loudly . . . anything to distract his attention.

'Joe, you should have spoken. You did

so much for me; you brought me up from nothing and gave me a chance to star. I haven't forgotten it; I never have forgotten, never could forget.'

He halted at that, and stood there, a shaking bundle of jelly. He looked ridiculous, but the girl saw only awful threat of pain and torment in that white hulk before her.

Perhaps he was thinking back to those Hollywood days, thinking of the days when he had been an up-and-coming film producer. Then he'd met Pet Deganya, had insisted on starring her in an important picture. And everyone had been right . . . she wasn't star material. The film was an expensive flop, a termination mark to his career.

Always neurotic, the vicious criticism, from the Press chiefly, had sent him in search of obscurity, and with hatred in his heart for most of mankind, tormentors ever. But he had followed Pet Deganya, his one passion in life, and finding her had joined forces with Maurice . . . Malta Maurice, and his gang.

He had found her, only to find she was

Maurice's girl friend. But he had joined Maurice, to be near her and with the vague hope that he would somehow win her someday. And to that end he had put his talents at the disposal of the gang, and he was very talented, as Hollywood had once recognised.

But though he had brought dizzying success to the gang, they had never shown respect for him in any way. He was a fat slug, something contemptible in everyone's eyes. Someone to be used and abused at the same time . . . the man who did the work . . . and got chiselled at every turn.

Pet was now a cheap little gangster's moll, always with a pert wisecrack on her carefully made up lips to get Maurice jeering at the butt of all their humour. Cheap . . . and yet he had gone on loving her.

Pet cried, 'Oh, Joe, how could you think it? I thought you liked fun.' And then she started to gabble, because suddenly she knew there was someone crouched outside under the window.

For just a second she had glimpsed

something that could only be the top of a man's head.

'You should have told me, Joe. How was I to know? You shouldn't have done what you did . . . '

Joe hadn't seen that movement behind him. He interrupted her. 'You mean, radio the police in the middle of that bank raid?'

He stormed at her, his unwholesome white face within inches of her own now, as she crouched up against the wall farthest from the window.

'Why shouldn't I do a thing like that? Why should I let Maurice have you? I hoped the police would catch them all, but they were too slow. I hoped they would get Maurice and all the gang and — and shoot them down like the rats they are. But they got away.'

'And then Maurice and his boys were after you for double-crossing them.' Her eyes started to stray over his shoulder. 'So you wrote that letter.'

A silly, hysterical letter that only an unbalanced man would write. Begging forgiveness for what he had done.

Forgiveness . . . from Malta Maurice! A man who had never done a thing in his life that was big and generous. A man who had chiselled and cheated, double-crossed and betrayed . . . a brutal man, mean and vindictive.

A silly letter. Offering to plan so many schemes to enrich the gang by way of retribution. As if Maurice could ever trust him again . . .

'You know why I wrote that letter?' Her eyes were on the window, but there was nothing to see. She kept on looking, hopefully. 'I wanted to be back near you, that's why I sent it. I couldn't bear to be away from you. My plan had failed and Maurice still had you. I was desperate enough for anything, just to get back to you.'

She was thinking: And Maurice gave his answer. Shot the man who went for that letter. It was the act of a man resorting to the utmost brutality out of reaction to the fear that had come to him during their narrow escape from the police. It was intended to demonstrate to the traitor that there could be no forgiveness, only bullets.

She brought her eyes back from the window, then saw that Joe Gell had noticed and was turning his fat white face that way. Frantically she thought of something to say. 'Maurice — you gotta watch out for him, Joe. I'm telling you as a friend. He's searching high and low for you, and he'll stick at nothing to find you. If he gets you, he won't be nice before you — die!'

She saw Joe Gell quiver, and it brought a little satisfaction to her that she had hurt him. Her leg felt bruised and tired, and she had a heavy feeling where her heart was tiredly beating.

Joe spoke, but kept his eyes on that window. 'He won't find me. He doesn't know I have this place. I haven't used it for years, not since before I went to Hollywood.' His eyes came round towards her. 'But I guess he'll be mad, all right.'

He paused, then said, abruptly, 'I guess I made him even more sore at me.'

Her eyes started to go towards the window, then stopped, afraid to betray her interest again. 'I don't understand, Joe?'

Joe sighed. 'Maurice always chiselled me out of my share. I never got anything, only promises. So I helped myself before I tipped off the police.'

'Meaning?'

'That gold bullion we got away with. It was stored away. I picked it up, and brought it with me.' His eyes were going round to that window again. Something seemed to have made him suspicious. Perhaps he had heard some sound from outside.

She tried to distract his attention. 'Joe — you've got me. What're you gonna do with me?'

He sighed. His so easily aroused passion seemed to have subsided. Bleakly he said, 'I don't know. All I knew was I couldn't leave you to — to Maurice. I had to get you away from him.'

His eyes looked beyond her, and they were hopeless, beaten. 'But now I've got you, I'm going to keep you — always. Even though I know you don't love me.' His voice became a whisper. 'I'm going to keep you tied up here, where no one will ever find you.'

He stopped; his head jerked towards the window, his body swaying, terror on his fat, white face. 'There's somebody outside,' he screamed. 'Maurice has found me. Oh, God!' And abruptly he lumbered across to the door and slammed out and into the passage. After a minute she heard a car start up and drive furiously away.

Relief flooded over her, and she started to cry again, then she sat up, but found there was that pain in her heart again. After a rest she levered herself slowly up against the wall, not putting any weight on the limb bearing those two close-fitting bracelets.

When she was upright she turned her soiled and woebegone little face towards the window.

Her eyes started to go wide, her mouth to open in a scream of horror.

For there was a man standing silently out there, looking at her.

A man without a face.

6

G-girl

The day that October Raine started with the F.B.I. a phone call came for Cheyenne Charlie. He wasn't there to take it. He hadn't been much in the office at all.

Once when he came in the chief said to him, 'You on to something?' because Cheyenne was moving around like a man with a purpose. He was also making the various Records men work for him.

Cheyenne's battered, copper-coloured face was non-committal. 'Maybe. I don't know yet. Maybe it's just a blind alley.'

'Well, what alley are you prowling up, you old Injun? Give!'

Cheyenne gave — a little. 'I'm thinking there's too much blond about this gang. It's overdone. It don't seem natural, chief. So I've stopped looking for blonds; instead I'm after dark-haired gents.'

The chief said, 'We had considered that

line, but it hadn't got us any place. So — what else?'

'I've got the maintenance boys working on a car which is known as the Chameleon.'

The chief stared.

'We're seeing how fast we can make a car change from bright yellow to dull black.'

The chief said, 'It takes us days . . . '

Cheyenne said, softly, 'It takes us seconds. We reckon to do it in a fraction of a second any time now.'

The chief nodded with satisfaction. Cheyenne seemed to be making headway. Cheyenne departed. It was while he was out that a message came from Fourth Precinct Police. It was typed out and kept until his return, then given to him with an explanation.

The chief said, 'That message was mailed to the police at Fourth Precinct yesterday. As we're on the case, the contents were immediately phoned through to us, but I have asked for the original letter to be brought along just as soon as they've gone over it for fingerprints.'

Cheyenne looked at the typed message, and his eyes widened. It read: 'Joe Gell killed Hicky Gue. Find him.' The signature read, 'The Blond Boys'.

Cheyenne said, 'That sure is interesting.' And then his brown eyes narrowed. 'Though mighty puzzling.' He looked suspiciously at the letter, instinct at work. 'There's something screwy about this letter . . . looks like a double-cross to me, chief.'

'In what way?'

Cheyenne wrinkled his nose. 'That message don't ring true, somehow, chief. It's that sentence . . . 'Find him', that seems wrong, somehow. You know what I think? I think these boys are trying to use the police as a catspaw.' He considered, then said, slowly, 'I think they're wanting Gell, badly, for some reason, but I think they don't know where to find him, so they've put the police on to his trail, hoping the cops'll find him for them.'

The chief said, complacently, 'Maybe if they knew the F.B.I. had moved in on the case they wouldn't have dared pull something like this.' But Cheyenne was thinking beyond that point.

'If that hunch is okay, chief, it suggests they've got big ears down at Fourth Precinct . . . and a big mouth to yap across with any information that comes through. They've got some cop in their pocket. It won't be the first time, I reckon.'

The chief was looking at another typed sheet. 'That's for you to consider, Chey. This is your job, and I'm only getting all the information I can for you.' He indicated the sheet before him. 'Immediately we received the message both we and the police made a search for Gell.'

'Find him?'

'No. And we haven't much on him, either. He seems to have disappeared in the last ten months. He was a small-time film producer with a New York company. Then he made a sensational film that carried him to Hollywood. After a couple of years there he produced one film that was such a stinker, he got fired. He left Hollywood for places unknown, and that's the last we've heard of him. He isn't back at his previous New York address, so we haven't been able to lay hands on him. We've sent out an all-stations call to pick him up, however.'

'Gell?' said Cheyenne. 'That Gell, huh? I remember the picture that made him famous. Wasn't it called, 'They Gave Him A Face'? Something about plastic surgery?' Cheyenne was remembering now. 'It was a brilliant bit of work . . . all faked, mind you, but really sensational.'

The chief said, 'There's only one other item of information. He was once reported to the police for the way he treated a girl assistant . . . his continuity girl. She didn't press the charge, so he got off. We're trying to trace her, but she seems to have disappeared, too.' He tossed the sheet across to Cheyenne.

Chey looked at the name and said, without turning a hair, 'That girl started working for the F.B.I. today,' and it brought the chief clambering up out of his chair in astonishment. Without asking permission, Cheyenne stabbed the intercom and barked to exchange . . . 'Find Miss October Raine and send her immediately to the chief's office.'

He was thoughtful, replacing the switch. 'What do you know about Miss October Raine?' he asked abruptly.

The chief said, 'Damn all. But someone will. She'd be well screened, I know. We'll find out for you. Why?'

Cheyenne shrugged. 'Guess I'm just a nasty, suspicious person. Probably there's nothing in the suspicion at all. But that girl was mighty anxious to join the F.B.I. She said she was after thrills, adventure. Okay, so she might. But . . . suppose she's not on the level?'

'Big ears?'

'Like they've got at Fourth Precinct. It could be.'

The chief depressed a key. 'While there's any suspicion we'll do everything we can to check on the lady.' He spoke to Appointments. After a few seconds he got his answer. 'Nothing's known against her at all. She seems smart, competent, completely on the level. She likes to be called October Raine, though October's not her real moniker.' He paused, then said, 'Not that I blame her for the change.'

Cheyenne was too much of a gentleman to ask what her real name was. Instead he said, 'All the same, we'll keep an eye on her for a while.'

A few minutes later there was a tap on the door, and October was shown in. She was carrying pad and pencil, but she looked rather scared at being summoned into the chief's room. She started when she saw Cheyenne sitting there, big, brown and unsmiling, and then she looked just a little more at ease, as if feeling she had a friend present.

The chief said, courteously, 'Won't you sit down, Miss Raine?' though it was a command and not a question. Then he looked across at Cheyenne, silently handing over to the special operator.

Cheyenne smiled. October smiled. It was a way of disarming her, so that his question would come as a bombshell.

He stopped smiling abruptly. Said, 'What do you know of Joe Gell?'

Then both men watched her, like dogs waiting for the nose of a rabbit to appear.

October sat as if petrified, and her face

slowly started to redden. Then she gulped and spoke.

'I don't know . . . much.'

'When did you last see him?'

She considered. 'Three to four years ago, when I was working with him.'

'And you haven't seen him since?'

She shook her head. And then she showed that she had spirit. 'Now let me ask you a question. What are you getting at?'

Cheyenne looked at her steadily for a second and then said, 'We're trying to trace Gell in a hurry . . . for something mighty important. We know you once knew him . . . '

'How?' But that reddening came to her face again. She was smart; she had guessed.

'Police records. You once started to charge him for assault, then changed your mind. So . . . back to where we were. Can you give us any lead as to his whereabouts?'

She shook her head. 'He went to Hollywood. And I only know that because I read it in the papers. He should have done well there, but his third picture was ghastly. For once in his life he got obstinate . . . insisted that an unknown girl got the lead in his new picture. She was just so bad it killed him. They had to re-shoot the whole darned story, pretty near, and that'd cost half a million bucks, I reckon.'

'He came back to New York.'

'I didn't know that.' She seemed to be honest enough in her answers. She was quite self-possessed now, too. A pretty, intelligent, modern Miss America. 'I haven't heard about him for ages.'

So Cheyenne admitted, 'I was only guessing that he had come back to New York. Now, G-girl, if you ever want to make a name in the force, rack your beautiful brain and think of a place where we might find him.'

October thought. Then admitted, 'The beautiful brain doesn't seem to function so well today.'

So, patiently, Cheyenne got to work to try to prompt her memory. He started to talk about Gell, hoping that from it all a note would sound that would bring forth an answering chord from her brain.

'Tell us about Gell. What sort of a fellar would you say he is? And try to be objective about your answers . . . forget anything wrong he's done to you.'

'He was brilliant, but didn't look it.' October was staring into the past. 'He knew his stuff as a film producer . . . there wasn't a subject he didn't seem expert on. And he seemed able to make anything; he was extraordinarily ingenious. But then you'll remember that film which made him famous . . . 'They Gave Him A Face'? It was the cleverest thing made for years.'

Cheyenne nodded. He remembered the film well; it wasn't all that long since it had been the rage of America.

October went on . . . 'I knew him well because for a time I was a continuity girl.'

'That job didn't last?'

She shrugged. 'What do you think, after I'd made a charge against him? I couldn't work near the slug after that. Anyway, almost immediately afterwards he got his big chance and went to Hollywood . . . and messed himself up by all accounts.'

'You don't seem complimentary about him. Why . . . slug?'

October turned her eyes towards the G-man. There was loathing in them. 'He makes me shudder, just thinking about him. He was the unhealthiest piece of manhood that ever walked.'

'Was?'

'Is, for all I know or care.' She went on to describe Gell. 'Bigger than you'd think when you got close to him, and heavy with fat. Revoltingly heavy. It seemed to hang in soft, lardy masses all over him, and his skin was deathly pale because he never seemed to go outside if he could help it. I think his eyes were bad and they made him shun sunlight.'

'A big man, huh? Strong?'

'Except for his hands, as soft as a kitten.'

'But could he, do you think, do something like . . . killing a man with a gun?'

October was derisive. 'Joe Gell? He was so craven he was afraid of his own shadow. I don't think Gell had the guts to do anything violent in all his life. Even when he was the big shot, the producer, everyone treated him like dirt. Jelly Joe everybody called him to his face, and right down to the callboy everyone jeered at him and made fun of his fat body and the funny ways he had. Everyone did it, knowing he would never have the guts to say anything about it. Everyone . . . except just a few. And I was one who got sick of it, because I was near to him and didn't think it fair, and sometimes I said so.'

'So?' October wasn't so easy now. She had paused, as if not wanting to enter on to the next subject, but Cheyenne's prompting reluctantly brought her to it. 'Well, I guess that's why he took to me a bit. I suppose I seemed less unfriendly than the other girls on the set.'

'So he made advances which you objected to?'

'He got me to go home with him one day, saying there was work for me to do. And then, when we were there, he got all soft and maudlin . . . he's a dreadful neurotic . . . and started telling me of all the things he would give me if I would only be friendly.' She shuddered. 'But he frightened me, and I ran away and kept on running until I met up with a motorist who took me to the nearest police station. Afterwards, when I'd time to think it over, I decided to forget about him. He was so screwy, he wasn't responsible, I reckoned.'

Cheyenne chewed over a sentence thoughtfully. 'I . . . kept on running until I met up with a motorist who took me to the nearest police station.' For some reason that didn't sound at all like New York.

Aloud he said, 'Where did he take you? His apartment out at Jersey?'

'Oh, no.' She seemed surprised. 'I thought I told you. He had a place somewhere in the Catskills . . . a summer lodge.'

'Honey,' said Cheyenne, 'why couldn't you come out with that ten minutes ago?' He was reaching for a phone, dialling.

October looked indignant, then remembered where she was and sat in silence, pouting because he hadn't treated her with dignity.

Cheyenne got through. It was to the Fourth Precinct's HQ. He seemed to know somebody there. He said, 'Get it around that the F.B.I. have already traced Joe Gell. He used to have a summer lodge in the Catskills. Whether he's out there or not doesn't matter . . . I want the police to believe he's still out there. Go through the motions of trying to trace the address for me, willya? You'll be able to get it from the local police.'

He paused, as if listening, and then said, 'Me? No, I don't want it. I'm going out there right away on a personally conducted tour. I guess I got someone here who'll find the place for me.'

Another pause, then, 'No, I still want you to find that address . . . and when you get it, don't keep it to yourself . . . Yes, that's it . . . You're dead right I think you've got a big mouth down there . . . No, I think he's gonna be mighty useful. So long.'

The chief lifted his eyebrows when Cheyenne replaced the receiver. 'What's that in aid of?'

'I'm preparing a trap. If my hunch is

correct, the Blond Boys want Joe Gell and they're looking to the police to find him for them. Okay, so I want to be out there ahead of them, to have a reception committee waiting when they turn up.'

He turned to October. 'You can powder your nose, honey. You're going with a lot of nice big G-men out to Joe Gell's joint.' At which October floored them by saying, meekly, 'I don't know where it is. It was so long ago, and I was taken by car.'

7

Cheyenne finds a corpse

Cheyenne said, 'Well, knock me for a home run. Who'd have thought that!'

Then the chief barked, 'Just think, Miss Raine. Think, girl, think. Try to remember some place you passed through, going out.'

October said, 'Dip . . . Dip . . . Dip something.'

The chief said, 'Mendip?' and the girl's face brightened. The chief turned to Cheyenne. 'Take her out with you to Mendip. I guess she'll find her way from there, all right.'

Cheyenne heaved his bulk off the chair. It sang a happy note of relief. 'I'll go ahead with the girl. Have your men in another car pick up my trail at Mendip. See they're armed . . . I've an idea we're gonna meet these Blond Boys, and it seems they go for tommies, nowadays.'

Then he whisked the girl down to the car park. As he went he gripped her arm and grinned, 'You wanted to be a G-girl. You're getting your chance a whole lot sooner that you thought, huh? How'd you like it?'

She was straight, confessed, 'Things have happened with such bewildering speed, I don't know what to make of it. Not sure I am enjoying it.' And then she asked, 'Are you armed?'

He nodded. 'I'm always armed. I don't feel dressed without a gun.' His hand stole up towards a shoulder holster.

Then they got into the car and Cheyenne headed out first west and then south. He knew the way to the Catskills but had to ask for the tiny hamlet of Mendip. When they came out of the woods and into the one solitary street, charming in its imitation New England style, they stopped off for coffee and some ham and eggs. Cheyenne parked the car in a conspicuous place.

After a time four big young men came in and sat down to a meal. Cheyenne looked at them once and was satisfied.

These would be the G-men sent after him. But no sign of recognition passed between them. It might be useful for Cheyenne and the girl to appear to be just a pair of tourists . . .

Their meal finished, Cheyenne walked out to his car. He was slow in starting up, in order to give the four huskies their chance of coming out, and afterwards he drove so that the second car had no difficulty in keeping them in sight.

There was no difficulty for the first mile . . . only one road ran out of Mendip. But then they came to a fork, and October had to do some thinking before plumping for the left turn. She had a feeling the hills way up left were familiar, so Cheyenne turned that way.

They were on the right track, because October spotted several familiar land-marks. Then she had to make several decisions in quick succession, and wasn't so happy.

Cheyenne felt her hand on his arm. 'Don't go any further. I think we must be very near, but I don't recognise this part of the road.'

They stopped and looked round. They were in a pleasant parkland, with good, well-farmed meadows, and plenty of trees on the rolling ground. One or two farmhouses showed up, but October shook her head and said none was familiar. Then Cheyenne saw a labourer hoeing a turnip field down the valley, and he started to get out of the car.

'Wait here,' he said. 'Maybe that fellar knows the Gell place. It'll be quicker than pottering around these lanes all night.' The afternoon sun was low and yellow over the western horizon now, and the air was beginning to be chilly at this height.

Cheyenne looked down the valley road and saw that the other car had parked unobtrusively a quarter of a mile back. He thought: They might just as well have come up alongside me, here, with no one around.

Then he nimbly vaulted a gate and went stiff-legged down the long slope to where the old man was working.

October got out of the car, too. She wanted to stretch her legs, as she had been sitting for far too long for her energetic spirit. She first clambered on to a tumbling wall that must have been built in the days of Paul Revere, and then on impulse jumped down and started to climb the bush-covered hill, hoping to spot Gell's house from this vantage point.

She wasn't at the top when a movement caught her eye. At that moment she was on all fours, clambering up a steep draw. Right ahead of her, where low bushes screened the head of the tiny valley, someone was crouching, looking down towards her.

Panting, she sat and watched. She couldn't see much, because the figure was partly hidden by the bushes, but there was something repellent about the stillness of the watching, crouching man, so she made no move to go forward.

After a minute, the figure stirred and came a little more into the open, but still she couldn't see much because of the screen of bushes. Couldn't see his face, that is. But she could see a ragged arm and a hand, and the hand was beckoning to her to come on, beckoning eagerly.

She shook her head. She didn't like the

situation at all. So the hand beckoned even more frantically . . . and there was something frantic in the gesture. But at that the girl turned and started to slide down the draw.

When she looked again, the man had disappeared, so she stopped where she was. She felt that from the top she might spot Gell's old place, but she wasn't going to risk walking into somebody's arms in those thick bushes. She waited for a couple of minutes or so, trying to decide.

And then she made her decision. To go back to Cheyenne and see how he had got on first. It was a bit late in the day to take risks . . .

Shivering, she turned. And looked down. At a man silently creeping up the draw from behind her. A scarecrow of a man.

And then he lifted his face, and she started to scream.

For he didn't have a face that she could see. Just a flat raw blankness, from which tiny eyes peered out and in which was a little black 'O' of a mouth.

He made funny mewing noises at her, and waved his hands ditheringly, and then he turned and plunged off through the bushes. She heard the crackling sound of his passage, and it reassured her and she took to her heels as fast as she could go down that steep slope.

Cheyenne had heard her scream and was running up to the car, followed much more slowly by the old man. October didn't wait when she got to the road; she ruined her nylons clambering over the gate, then pelted down towards that comforting big G-man.

Cheyenne shouted. 'What's the matter, girl?' But October simply took off, five yards away, and leapt into his arms.

And then seconds had to pass before she could get her breath and tell him, minutes before her fright left her. And she had had a scare, Cheyenne could see.

The old man arrived in time to hear her story. He was as thin as a runner bean stem, and nearly as lanky; a warped, stooped, dirt-coloured old timer with a billy-goat beard and no teeth above it. The sort of old boy you'll find tending turnips in every State west of Massachusetts, where they don't go in much for beards.

Cheyenne exclaimed, 'What the hell, you bin scared by a man without a face! Now, what sort of a story is that to give a fellar?'

She sobbed, 'It's true, Charles. He was there, crouched up among those bushes, beckoning to me to go up to him. And when I turned to come back to the car, he'd worked round me and was right there in front of me. And I tell you, he hadn't a face . . . not what you'd call a face, anyway!'

Cheyenne looked doubtful. 'A man without a face, huh? Now, what's this mean?'

The old man was making mouth noises preparatory to speech. It came out. 'Guess the gal ain't stretchin' truth at that, mister. Guess there is a fellar hangs aroun' this place, an' he ain't got no face to speak of, neither.'

He licked bloodless old lips with a thin, pointed tongue that flickered in and out like a rattlesnake's, then went cackling on

. . . 'He's bin known to us for a coupla years or more. Don't do no one no harm, so we don't bother with him none. Guess he's mighty sensitive of that face o' his'n, 'cause he don't show hissel' more'n he c'n help.'

He squirted thin spittle during a ruminative pause, then said, 'He musta got some place fixed back in them woods, though nobody don't seem to know where. Must be mighty cold in winter.' Another spit. 'Most times I see him he's a-hangin' round that place you were enquiring on.'

'Gell's?' interposed Cheyenne quickly.

'Him . . . that film man.' That craggy goat head nodded, and then a wicked gleam came into the old eyes. There was life in the old dog yet. 'He don't like men . . . allus runs away from 'em . . . but lately he's started follerin' women. He don't do nothin', jes' tries to 'tice 'em into the bushes. Must be kinda lonely in them woods, I guess.' He gave vent to a cackling laugh.

They thanked the old boy for his information, said goodbye, and watched him totter off to his hoe. Then they climbed up to the car.

Starting up, the special operator said, 'He remembers Gell . . . the film man, he was known as round here. Says Gell's place has stood empty since he went to Hollywood. It's back up the next valley.' He indicated the shoulder of hill that October had tried to climb.

The girl shuddered. 'Charles, you must have your big, broad shoulders close to mine when we go there! That wicked old man said my latest admirer hung around the Gell place a lot . . . I want you to be around if we meet up with him again.'

Cheyenne turned the car. He had intended stopping alongside the second F.B.I. car, but several automobiles were coming up the road now, and so he didn't risk it. Instead, as they passed he gave a slight signal to follow. He saw the squad car turn and come behind them. Then he gave his attention to the approaching cars.

But they just roared past. They were big cars, city cars, but there was nothing suspicious about them. Most contained a woman or women in addition to any menfolk, and only these women were blonde, and none of the men.

Down the valley they turned up a side road that was winding and bumpy between tall hedgerows.

October said, 'Charles.'

He took one hand off the wheel. It was a big hand and looked even bigger now because it was clenched. He said,: unemotionally, 'You call me Charles again and I'll rattle the teeth in that pretty head for you. Call me Charlie, or Chey, or Cheyenne, like even the chief does when he forgets. *But don't call me Charles, get me?*'

'Why not?' she pouted. 'It's a nice name.'

'It's the name for a cissy,' he told her.

Shamelessly she snuggled closer to him. 'You ain't no cissy . . . Cheyenne,' she told him, and she stayed snuggled up to him and he didn't raise any objection. It felt nice to him, the scent rising from her hair. It felt even nicer to the girl, that comforting strength after the scare she'd had . . .

The Gell place wasn't hard to find. They came over a sudden brow on the hill road, and saw it back against some dark evergreens. Cheyenne pulled up and looked at it hard.

Then he took the car out of gear and coasted off the road so that his vehicle was screened by bushes. He said, 'I saw something move, back of the house. I'm goin' up on my own. You sit there and wait till I come back.'

He started to walk. When he looked the girl was trotting at his side. He said, 'I told you to stay in the car.'

'Like heck I'll stay,' was her terse reply. 'Think I'm gonna stay there by myself with Faceless Freddie wandering around? Mister, you've got yourself a shadow.'

Cheyenne shrugged. It didn't seem to matter much. At any moment, anyway, the squad car would be along, to wait unobtrusively within calling distance. He took her arm and grinned. 'Okay, then we'll march openly up to the door, you and I. Our story is we've lost our way; could we please be directed back to Mendip? That is, if anyone wants our story.'

They were marching up to the house now, arm in arm, making, as October remarked, a very affectionate picture.

Cheyenne was thinking that the squad car seemed rather a long time in coming over that brow.

But to the girl . . . 'We'll complete the story by saying we're honeymooning, huh? I haven't had a honeymoon for a long time; guess I could do with one now.'

His eyes were looking back of the house, among those evergreen shrubs and tall, dark spruce and larch trees. He had seen a movement there when he stopped the car. Only a brief movement, a vision of something white among the trees; but it had set him wondering.

It could be that sick-mind, the faceless guy, of course. But then, equally, it could be someone else, like the Blond Boys.

He heard October saying softly, 'Did you notice something about what the old man said to you? About Faceless Freddie being first seen in this district just about the time Gell went away?'

'Meanin'?' Cheyenne halted, short of the front door, blistered by the sun and eroded by fierce winter gales.

'Meanin', maybe there's some connection between them, somehow. For why should he hang around the Gell place so much, anyway?'

Cheyenne shrugged. 'You tell me.' He had decided not to knock on the front door immediately. He thought he'd like to have a peep through one of the windows, first.

He slipped quietly across the overgrown flowerbeds that were knee high with weeds, then stopped abruptly, looking down. Someone else had done some slipping across this way before him . . . the weeds were flattened and bruised and presented their upturned silvery undersides to him.

He followed the tracks and they led direct to the window he had been looking at. Then he realised that the girl was hard behind him.

Alongside the window he paused and glanced quickly round. Over this part of the valley there was dead silence, apart from the furtive rustling of those sombre dark trees behind the house. He felt

October shiver, pressing up to him. She didn't like the atmosphere of the place.

He pushed her away and silently tapped his shoulder holster. She understood. He might need to go for his gun any time now, and he wouldn't want her in the way of a quick draw.

Then he started to edge round so that he could look into the window.

All at once someone moaned. For a second Cheyenne imagined it was the girl and turned sharply to look at her. But it wasn't October. Then the moaning started again, and he knew that it came from inside that room.

He pulled his eye around the corner.

The room was fairly large, and there was not much furniture in it. But what drew Cheyenne's attention was a long, heavy workbench against the far wall, and built on to the wall appeared to he some sort of simple electrical control panel.

All this his eyes saw in a first swift photographic glance. Then his attention rested on the two occupants of the room.

A man, kneeling. And a woman lying sprawled on the floor.

Cheyenne didn't need to be told . . . that woman was dead. There was something in that grotesque posture of limbs that told the story.

Then the man looked up and saw the G-man. Cheyenne saw a big, fat moon-face, deathly white and eyes staring through thick-lensed glasses. The moaning stopped. With surprising agility the white-faced man panicked and fled out of the room.

Cheyenne started to sprint round to the back to intercept him, but the girl was standing right at his shoulder and he nearly flattened her with his impulsive movement and almost fell on to his face himself.

He regained his balance and plunged round the house-end. Back of him came a frantic pattering of feet. October Raine wasn't going to be left far behind.

But the going wasn't easy, round the corner. Here thorn bushes had built up a barrier and Cheyenne lost minutes in trying to find a way through them. When they came out on to a paved yard with an old-fashioned pump in it, they knew that the white-faced man had got away. High up among the spruce and larches they could here the crashing of some heavy body.

There was a door swinging open leading into the house. Cheyenne looked at it, undecided. Then he looked up at the thick wood and rapped, 'A fat guy, soft and unwholesome like a new-hatched grub. Big white face and glasses. Nervous as hell. Know him?'

October Raine said promptly, 'Joe Gell . . . or he's got himself a stand-in.'

Cheyenne nodded. 'Then he can wait. We'll pick up a guy like that any time we want.'

He headed for the door, and October jumped into action after him. Those dark trees looked very sinister, and it wasn't Joe Gell she was afraid of.

They went along a passage that stank damp and mouldy, and Cheyenne threw open doors to see what lay beyond. But he didn't need to open the door of the death chamber. That was already open wide, a silent invitation for them to enter.

Cheyenne hurried into the room, saw

the huddled body on the floor and dropped beside it. One glance at that ghastly, fear-drawn face, rigid in death, was enough.

'Dead,' he muttered. 'And for some hours, if not days.' Then he remembered October, remembered she was a girl and mightn't be used to such sights.

October's face was pale, but she was sticking it well. He said, 'You don't need to look if you don't want. But if you can tell me anything about the girl it might help.'

He was on his knees, careful not to disturb anything, yet examining the body for injury. But he didn't see any.

The girl forced her voice into steadiness. 'I wouldn't be sure, but her face looks familiar. I think it's Pet Deganya, a film actress.'

'More association with film-land,' said Cheyenne. He was looking at an electric cable that ran back to the wall. Followed it to the girl's leg and saw that one end terminated on a broad steel band that was clamped to the naked skin, Then saw that another wire ran to a second band clamped around a bare ankle.

October went on, 'You don't seem to understand. Pet Deganya was the actress who put an end to Joe Gell's Hollywood career.'

Cheyenne looked up quickly. 'That one? The girl he pushed into a leading part, only to find she couldn't act worth anything, huh?'

October nodded. Cheyenne squatted back on his haunches. He was looking at that cable and switchboard. He was thinking: It could be someone gave the girl a shock, and she died from it. That blueness to the face could indicate heart failure brought on by shock of this nature. Aloud he said, 'Maybe Joe Gell was sore at the girl for letting him down so. Maybe he fixed up some crazy revenge scheme. You tell me, honey . . . could Joe Gell torture a girl?'

She thought for some time. At last she shook her head. 'I'd be surprised if he did. He didn't seem to have any guts. When he started to make up to me that time, he was terrified, all the time he was doing it. And I didn't have to struggle very hard to get away from him.'

Without thinking, Cheyenne wisecracked, 'Maybe that wasn't very complimentary to your charms, honey.' And October thought him callous with that dead girl lying there. Which was wrong. Cheyenne was used to death . . . it was part of his trade. That was all.

The special operator went on, slowly, 'You'd be surprised what gutless creatures do at times. When a gutless person does anything, he usually does it in a big way. Some of the most brutal crimes I've investigated have been committed by little, hen-pecked men who haven't said boo to a goose or to their wives during their whole life.'

October was suddenly looking down the passage.

Cheyenne rose. Best thing would be to go out and signal for the squad car to approach. He was saying, 'That's the way it is, honey. You get kicked around all your life until one day you can't stand it any more. Then you kick back, and in that kick you try'n put everything you've ever suffered. Maybe Joe Gell did just that.

Maybe though, he didn't really intend to kill the girl but gave her a shock that stopped the old heart . . . '

October was squeezing his hand.

His eyes came up slowly. A gun barrel was pointing at his heart. Back of that gun barrel was a drawn-back bolt and a magazine that could hold twenty .45 bullets. A sub-machinegun.

And holding it, looking in at the window at him, was a big blond man with a curious deadpan face.

8

The Blond Boys

Cheyenne didn't make any false move. They weren't taught heroics in the Service, and the special operator knew all about tommy guns . . . knew, for instance, that no action of his could ever beat that curled trigger finger.

He stayed stiff, rigid, because he wanted to go on living. Then he felt that squeeze on his hand again, and his head came slowly round.

He saw the wide, startled eyes of the girl and followed them.

Men were moving slowly up the passage towards them. Four or five of them. And the leading man carried a tommy, while the others had revolvers in their hands.

And all were as blond as the man outside the window, all had the same deadpan features.

They came silently to the door and stood looking in. Cheyenne obliged by raising his hands without being told.

All those narrow-eyed men were looking at him, all except one who was staring down at the girl on the floor.

There was not a flicker of animation on the deadpan countenance, but all the same somehow Cheyenne got the feeling of considerable emotion from the one man looking down at the contorted body. The G-man was looking hard at those faces, trying to understand . . .

Everyone stood in silence for a few seconds, and then that blond deadpan who had been staring down at the girl, slowly lifted his head and Cheyenne looked into dark brown eyes that were brimming with hate and ruthless ferocity.

Before the G-man knew what was happening, the Blond Boy jerked his hand up . . . hard. And it was the hand that carried an automatic. Cheyenne rode the blow a little, but most of the weight was transposed through that hard metal into his face. Tears scalded, and he tasted blood. But he didn't go down. He recoiled back against the wall and stood facing them.

October cried with horror when the blow was struck, but then abruptly she went silent and stood and watched them.

The Blond Boy snarled, 'That'll show you we mean business, bud!'

Cheyenne was listening for betraying accents. They came. He was satisfied.

'Now, talk,' grated the Blond Man. Cheyenne was beginning to get an idea he was leader of this mob. 'Who are you? What're you doin' here? What d'ya know 'bout this . . . ?' indicating the late Pet Deganya.

Cheyenne looked at the threatening front of men, silent, hard, their eyes merciless. But his story was ready. 'I'm Matt Charles . . . Matthew Charles. I'm a dry-goods salesman from Oakland, Cal. We're honeymoonin' in New York an' we came out for the day to see the Catskills. We missed our way, so we stopped off here to get put right. We saw something was wrong when we looked through this window . . . saw this girl and a fellar kneeling over her . . . '

'What was he like?' There was hard suspicion in the low, growling voice, suspicion of everything that Cheyenne was saying.

Cheyenne replied, 'He was a fat, awkward slob, with a fat, white face and glasses.' Then he worked up to indignation. 'And now, what'n the hell d'you mean by bustin' in my face like that? Who the hell are you, anyway? You got nothin' on me . . . '

The chief Blond Boy snarled, 'Shut your face!' Then he turned to his followers. They talked softly, but Cheyenne heard quite a lot.

The chief snarled, 'It's Gell. He done this, you c'n see. That's another thing we owe him. When he goes out, it's gonna be slow, mighty slow.'

There was something said by one of the men that Cheyenne didn't gather; then the chief was saying, 'It might be here. We'll look for it . . . now. Watch this guy closely; he got that face with fightin'.'

He crossed to a second door that led direct on to some other room. It wasn't locked, but it opened to the turn of the handle with considerable protests. And as it opened there was a tearing sound, as cobwebs parted.

One of the Blond Boys looked at the dirty webs and said, 'That don't happen in a week, boss. Reckon that door's not bin used for years.'

They were looking into a room that clearly must once have been a library. It was lined with shelves supporting thousands of dropping, decaying volumes, and there was a desk in the centre of the room and a few chairs.

But everywhere were cobwebs. Cheyenne hadn't seen so many in years. Even the windows were dimmed with spreading webs.

The Blond Boys walked into the room. On an impulse Cheyenne went in with them, and then was stopped close by the door. The chief looked at the dust over everything, then crossed to another door. He didn't bother to open it. It was bolted from inside, and was cobwebbed, too.

He looked around and cursed. He seemed badly disappointed. 'It ain't here,' he growled. 'That's certain. No one c'n have bin here in months. Better look the house over, quick. There was that car with the flat back down the road. Them huskies had cops written all over 'em.'

He was nervous, wanted to be away. He started to hurry to the door, when one of the men asked, 'What're we gonna do with the bride an' groom?'

The chief snapped, 'Search 'em. Check on their story. An' if they ain't on the up-an'-up ... ' He went out without finishing his remark, but it didn't sound pleasant.

One of the Blond Boys made Cheyenne turn his back to him while he frisked him. Cheyenne had noticed that before, that the Blond Boys never came up near, or let him get a close view of them ...

They found his gun. 'What's this for? Dry-goods peddlers don't carry guns.'

Cheyenne saw the anxiety on October's face. He rapped back, 'Some o' the goods I peddle ain't strictly dry.' He made it sound like some racket he was on. 'A gun comes in handy once in a while.'

They got his wallet out. Cheyenne saw

October's pretty face go white with dread. He wanted to reassure her, but couldn't very well.

She watched while they looked at his licence and a Government identification permit, and several letters She was thinking: Any moment now they'll shoot him. They'll see he isn't Matt Charles . . .

But they didn't shoot him. They just grunted when they'd finished and shoved the wallet back into his suit coat pocket, and one of them growled, 'Seems okay. Everythin' checks.'

She nearly gave the show away with her sigh of relief. Then she looked up and caught the G-man's eye . . . and understood. There was a glint of humour on that big, battered pan, and she knew then that Matt Charles was always prepared for a search.

The only thought in Cheyenne's mind just then was that it was lucky he carried his F.B.I. badge in a secret little pocket right behind the centre button of his suit coat. For it was curious, that when a guy was frisked they didn't pay much attention to the front.

If October felt relief it wasn't long-lived. For the same Blond Man said, 'It's gonna be tough for the pair of them anyway. The boss won't want to turn 'em loose.'

There was a lot of suggestion behind that unfinished sentence. Cheyenne said nothing, but cursed cars that develop flats at critical moments. Then he thought: That won't matter much. They'll have a new wheel slapped on in minutes. So long as they don't miss this place, that's all.

He looked at the window. He thought that other Blond Boy with the sub-machinegun would still be out there. He was thinking: Perhaps right now the squad car's sittin' in ambush, waitin' for 'em to show outside again. Only he didn't feel too confident. The trail had been broken and now it might take some time to pick it up again.

A few minutes later the rest of the Blond Boys came back to the room. No one appeared to look at the corpse on the floor any longer; even the chief seemed wrapped up in some other anger. He came in swearing.

Cheyenne thought: Whatever it was they hoped to find, they haven't succeeded. He wondered what it could be.

And then a gun fired off. A single shot. And then another . . . a burst.

Cheyenne saw that deadpan face swing round towards him, heard a snarl. 'A trap!' Then a gun started to come up, and, too late, he threw himself desperately through that open library door.

All in a fraction of a second. October was clinging to that gun arm. The gun blazed, but the girl's weight had pulled the barrel down and the bullet merely furrowed the carpet.

Cheyenne, rolling, heard an echo of the blast in the room where he had come diving. One of the volume-filled shelves . . . a bottom one . . . had collapsed and the books were spilt on to the floor. He thought: The place must be rotten, and rolled quickly on to his feet. Instinctively his hand started to go for his shoulder holster. Then he remembered it would be empty.

Back in the room, the chief swung October away with a brutal backhander, then turned and raced out through the back door. Cheyenne, bunching for an attack, saw the girl smack against a wall with a force that must have taken the breath from her body, then she slid down and rolled over just by the door.

The last of the Blond Boys was belting after the chief. He was half-turned, ready to loose off a bullet at Cheyenne, framed now in the doorway, when he started to run on air and he kept on running until his face grazed the floor of the passageway. Cheyenne saw October's small oval face, saw her blonde hair all tousled and awry now, saw big blue eyes staring. Then saw her outstretched leg and understood.

She tripped him!

But the exultation came while he was in mid-air, launched head first in a flying attack. He wanted to get hands on one of the Blond Boys . . .

That fellar was recovering rapidly. A big bozo. He was bouncing up on to his feet all in one movement, and that gun hadn't left his tight-gripped hand.

Then Cheyenne crashed into him, and began to choke the life out of him, and he did it coldly, expertly — meaning to. The gunman screamed.

Another fifteen seconds and Cheyenne would have broken that neck; because this was no time for half-measures. He wanted one opponent out of the way, and he wanted that gun.

Instead he got bullets. Tommy gun lead.

That scream had caught the attention of the strong-arm boy with the sub-machinegun. He stopped and fired from the hip. At that range the only thing that saved Cheyenne was the fact that the gunner couldn't aim at him for fear of exterminating his comrade. But Cheyenne knew within seconds that the gunner would be able to pick his target and that target would be Charlie Chey, Special Operator.

So Cheyenne kicked viciously, as hard as he could, hoping to incapacitate the Blond Boy and leave him cold. But instead his knee caught bone.

Cheyenne rolled back into the room, rolled against something. Heard the roar of machinegun fire out in the passage and saw the cascade of plaster that followed. Then he realised that he had rolled against the dead Pet Deganya, silently, sightlessly staring out on the scene.

Cheyenne kicked the door shut as he rolled away. He didn't go in front to lock, but stood there, to one side, gesturing to October to keep out of range in case they gave a burst through the door itself.

But no shooting followed. Instead they heard feet pounding out the back way. For a few seconds after the runners had left the house, there was silence. Then firing started again outside. October ran across to the detective, and he put his arm round her.

He squeezed her, said, 'Attagirl. That was good work. Now book me for assault.' He gave her a kiss. It wasn't the sort of kiss most fellars would give a girl. This was something a bit like a wrestling hold and with a force behind it that could have been a knockout punch.

When he was through she couldn't breathe. Big Cheyenne said, complacently, 'That's your reward, honey, for saving my life.'

October got her breath, and said weakly, 'I promise I'll never do it again.' She shoved him away, then hugged her ribs. They were nice ribs, or had been until Cheyenne got around them. She felt bruised all over, then charitably decided to put only half down to Cheyenne's embrace and give the other half to contact with a hard wall.

She looked round, carefully avoiding looking at the late Pet Deganya. She was amazed. 'Aren't you going after them?'

He said coolly, 'You c'n go, if you like.'

October swung back the door and went to look into the passage. Cheyenne picked her up by her collar and lifted her back into the room — just in time.

A solitary pistol shot crashed out in the passage and more plaster showered down. Then someone started to run out the back way, too.

Cheyenne said, 'It's automatic. You kick a fellar where I kicked him, and even if it doesn't land quite where you want it, it still hurts. Boy, and how it hurts! So the fellar just hangs around a coupla seconds and hopes to God he'll be able to ease the pain with some lead in the fellar that kicked him. That's experience tells me all these things.'

The girl said, indignantly, 'Why didn't you tell me he was there, then?' She was badly shaken.

But Cheyenne wasn't listening to her. He had crossed the window and was peering out. The automatic fire seemed to have receded.

The G-man nodded with satisfaction, squinting round the corner of the window. 'Good Boys,' he murmured. 'They did right, that time.' And to the girl he explained, 'They've got the Blond Boys' car covered. They can't get away by road.' He listened again to the firing. He thought: They know it, too. They're takin' a powder over the hilltop.

Then he showed himself at the window, because he could see one of the squad men doubling across, suspicious of the house. Cheyenne saw the gun hand go up, and he dropped to the floor just as the window smashed above his head.

October gasped, 'Who did that?'

'One of my boys.' Cheyenne was nonchalant. There hadn't been any danger; he'd been ready for the mistake. 'He thought I was one of the Blond Boys left in the house, I guess.'

He ran out through the back way, and the girl followed, Cheyenne saw a path winding up among the trees, and his trained eyes saw soil disturbances and he knew that the men had run this way, so he followed. The girl called to him to slow down, but he didn't want her with him, anyway, so he kept right on.

There was no firing now. Cheyenne guessed that the men were escaping as hard as they could go.

The path led steeply upwards, and Cheyenne at last started to blow. But he kept up the pace; he knew that city crooks were more likely to find it hard work than he.

Once the wood thinned and he was able to look down into the clearing by the roadside where the house lay, he saw three men closing in on the house. It was good tactics; against machineguns, the best move was for them to keep the crooks away from their car. If he knew the squad men they'd already have put lead into its tyres.

Down left of him some noise came to his ears. That would be the fourth squad man, forcing his way through the thick undergrowth. Because he had found that easy-to-follow pathway, Cheyenne had already climbed well above him.

Only, Cheyenne was unarmed. He couldn't forget that, and as he went on he didn't relax his caution.

But the trail led right on over the neck. The crooks were intent only on making as much speed as possible. They had walked into a trap, and had been lucky to get away with it. If that tyre hadn't given out, the squad men would have been nicely posted to cripple the Blond Boys the moment they walked into the trap. As it was, there was still a chance of capturing them. By now one of the squad men would be back at the car radio, sending out an all-stations call, giving a description of the men . . .

Right on top of the hill Cheyenne started swearing. It wasn't ordinary cusswords, either, but best vintage language acquired from contact with San Francisco's waterfront.

For he realised that the G-man would send out a wrong description of the men.

9

Where is October Raine?

He hesitated, there on top of the brow. For a moment he almost decided to plunge back to the radio car and send out an amended description. And then he caught a glimpse of something moving in the distance and he decided to keep right on the trail. Sooner or later he would meet up with a phone and would be able to get a call through.

The way was downhill now, between bushes because the trees had ended just below the skyline, in the shelter of the sloping hill. And Cheyenne began to realise that a lake of considerable size lay ahead.

He also saw in the distance a number of sailing vessels, and heard the crackle of motor-exhausts and thought there must be a village or town on the edge of the lake somewhere just out of sight.

The path led out on to a road . . . a dirt road, true, but one obviously much more used than that pathway. Even as he was thinking this, another little thought crept into his mind. It didn't flower, as thoughts should, but just stayed there, to be pulled out and looked at some time later.

Cheyenne looked along the dirt road and saw signs, they weren't much, but they told Cheyenne all he wanted to know. His men had run north along the lakeside road. He glanced across the dirt road. That path continued straight on towards a bay in the lake.

Cheyenne went running up the road. He ran much more cautiously now, because he presented a good target out there in the comparative open. But no one opened fire on him.

He must have lost a lot of time over the next mile so that he witnessed the tragedy from afar, unable to interfere.

The road climbed a ridge, so that the wide, blue lake lay bathed in sunshine below and to his left, while farmland sloped down into a broad valley on his right. He came out above a steep cliff and looked down upon a collection of houses that nestled close to it for protection. He guessed one would be the principal farmers house while the others would be cottages to house his men.

But . . . and it was the tragedy of it . . . most of the men were spread out on those fields across the valley. Or perhaps after all it was better they were out of the way.

Cheyenne spotted the Blond Boys. They had left the dirt track and had taken a side trail down to the houses. He wondered why, then thought: An auto! The Blond Boys had to risk meeting people in order to get their sole chance of escape . . . a car.

On an impulse Cheyenne didn't run down after them but kept on running up to the edge of the cliff. He was unarmed, and didn't want to run into the Blond Boys' arms down there among the houses, and he thought that up here he would be able to shout a warning, perhaps, or get someone to use a telephone.

Some women came to the doors when the Blond Boys ran up. Cheyenne could see the mobsters plainly now. There were seven of them. The last man ran as if in pain, and he wondered if it was the result of a kick from a G-man that was crippling him.

It must have looked menacing, all those blond deadpans running suddenly upon the peaceful little hamlet. Or perhaps some woman saw and recognised the guns they carried. A shrill cry of alarm floated up to Cheyenne, almost on the cliff edge now, and he saw the bright dresses of the women the moment before doors hurriedly closed on them.

The Blond Boys posted themselves strategically about the hamlet, one tommy gunner covering the open space before the house, another gunman going round to the back. Then two parties went exploring. After a time there was a shout, and Cheyenne heard an engine starting. He groaned. He had hoped there wouldn't be a car down there.

Then he saw it coming lurching up from an outshed. It was a big, powerful car, though a bit old. Cheyenne thought it was just the car for the gang.

A man came out of one of the houses, shouting. And behind him was a woman, trying to drag him back. Cheyenne, above, heard his irate voice roaring in indignation, but it didn't stop the gang.

The sentries came running back and climbed into the car. Then that obstinate old man ran in front of it and stayed there with arms outstretched.

They ran him down. The driver didn't hesitate, didn't use his horn. It was completely and callously an act of deliberate intent.

The old boy was standing shouting, one moment; the next he was clinging to the front of the car and being pulled down under it. He started to scream when the weight came on to his legs, and then he stopped as the heavy wheel crushed over his body. It was the woman who was screaming now.

Cheyenne saw the car turn right, to climb up above the cliffs along ahead of him, and he started to run. Then he saw a farm worker running heavily across a field, attracted no doubt by the screams and the shooting. The man ran down a slope and began to climb a barbed wire fence just as the car came roaring round a bend. He was climbing carefully, as men do when they are trying to negotiate barbed wire. He couldn't have done anything to that car, perched where he was.

But as it raced past someone let fly with a machine-gun, and Cheyenne saw the body jerk as the lead smashed home. Then the body slumped and hung tangled up between the strands of barbed wire, and the sight looked familiar to the G-man . . . like sights he had seen too often out in the Pacific war.

The car pulled out on to the dirt track, about a quarter of a mile ahead of him. They must have seen him, perhaps recognised him, but they weren't bothered about him now, with a car under their feet.

They were much more bothered by a telephone line that ran on high posts alongside the road. Cheyenne saw the car stop, saw a gun barrel point out of a window, upwards. It stabbed flame . . . three times. And then the car raced off.

When Cheyenne got to the post the line had been shot through. Worse, only one side had come down from the insulator.

If both ends had fallen, he could have connected them, so that the phone back in the farmhouse would have got through . . .

The Blond Gang sped away, satisfied that they had made the best of a bad job. Sure now that the police would not pick them up, because they had confidence in Joe Gell's technique.

If they had known that Charlie Chey, special operator, already knew most of Joe Gell's technique they would not have felt so easy in their minds. And it would have been better if they had turned back, losing time though they did so, and hunted the G-man to death.

Because he was the one man who knew their secret, and it would have gone out with him. That is, excluding Joe Gell. But then by this time Joe Gell didn't count for much.

It seemed miles to the lakeside village, and Cheyenne was feeling flat out when he got there. When he was coming on to the concrete shore road before the houses, hotels and gaily painted cafés, a motor-cyclist came roaring up to meet him.

It was a cop, and he was a very suspicious cop at that. He stopped, twenty yards away from the approaching G-man. His goggles were shoved back, and Cheyenne realised that there was a gun resting on the tank just below his ungloved hand. That cop was ready for action.

The cop shouted, 'Stay where you are. Tell me, who are you, and why are you running?'

Wearily Cheyenne halted and lifted up his hands. He gasped back, 'I'm an F.B.I. operator.' The cop didn't move. So Cheyenne shouted, 'The hell, man, do I look blond? The hell, if I was a Blond Boy, would I come galloping into a village like I was doin'?'

So the cop let him approach and saw the shield on the leather plaque, and after

136

that he took the orders. Cheyenne swung a leg over the pillion, saying, 'Get me to the nearest phone.'

As they tore along, Cheyenne shouted, 'Did you see a big car with seven men in it go by just now?'

The cop shook his head. 'Only one car came by. It was from Cliff Bottom Farm. There was two guys in it. Didn't look to see who was drivin', but guess it would be the old man or his sons. I was lookin' for Blond Boys.'

Cheyenne shouted, 'They were in that car, I guess most of 'em were lying outa sight.' Stealing that car had been a lucky break for the mob.

They stopped off at the first café. Cheyenne ran in and grabbed the phone back of the counter. Everybody looked up, startled and surprised as the big, sweating F.B.I. man started triggering impatiently for exchange, and then a red-faced cop came hurrying in.

Cheyenne got through. Rapped, 'Police? This is F.B.I. Put out an all-stations alert for seven members of the Blond Gang, escaping in an old black sedan stolen from

Cliff Bottom farm. Only . . . don't look for blond this time. Look for seven very dark men, Italian-lookin' guys.'

He heard the cop gasp at his elbow as he replaced the receiver. So he explained, 'By now they're no more blond than I am.' And Cheyenne's Indian ancestors hadn't met up with a blond in a thousand years.

Then Cheyenne strode out between the tables of gaping people and stood looking along the concrete highway that wound off towards New York. It was no good getting a car and trying to catch up with them now; they had too good a lead for that.

So Cheyenne sighed and said to the cop, 'Guess I'd better get back to the Gell place . . . and the corpse. And this time my feet say they're gonna ride, at least most of the way.'

The cop said, 'If you go by road you'll have to go right round to Mendip, a hell of a way. But I could get someone to ferry you across the lake and it won't take you long to drop down into the valley from the other side.'

Cheyenne said, wearily, 'It sounds fine. I know my way down the other side.' He thought, 'It'll be downhill and not far. Reckon my dogs won't bark too much at that.'

The cop gave him a lift along to a young fellow he knew with a fast, white, cabin cruiser. The young fellow was entertaining two or three friends. Two of them were bright young college girls. Cheyenne decided there was something in cabin cruising, and then they reminded him of October Raine. For some reason suddenly he felt uneasy.

Suddenly he had a premonition that something had happened to the girl . . .

The boy shouted, 'Sure, sure. You're welcome, copper. Get your lazy self outa that seat, Beth, an' give it to the poor tired G-man.'

Cheyenne came aboard, didn't argue about taking the padded seat that the slim-limbed Beth willingly gave up. And the youth started up the engine and gave it the gun.

They creamed across the blue lake under the sunshine, sometimes the wind bringing a thin cooling spray to their faces. It was exhilarating, but it didn't last long. The youth at the helm seemed to know where to land Cheyenne, and he brought the boat into a bay that narrowed into a long, winding creek.

Here the woods crept up to the edge of the water, and trees overhung the creek. The ground looked marshy on either side, and the place stank a bit. They negotiated the ribs of a rotted vessel that just showed in the channel. Here and there they also saw vessels moored in the more pleasant side creeks, and there was one beached and lying on its side.

Beth, hair streaming, shouted, 'They got no sense, tyin' up there. The mosquitoes come out of the water in millions and bite you to death.'

The youth shouted, 'She should know. She's tried every place . . . an' with a different fellar each time.'

Cheyenne jumped ashore and left the kids still arguing about 'the best place'. He had more serious problems on his mind than necking.

He was challenged when he came

running down that steep path amoi spruce and larch trees. A G-man denly showed round a tree trunk, gun at the ready. Then he must have recognised the special operator, for he put down the gun and stepped out into the open.

Cheyenne said, 'You can stop playin' boy scouts among the trees, brother. The Blond Boys are miles away now in a stolen car.'

They walked down to the house together. None of the G-men had been hurt. Cheyenne walked across to the Blond Gang's black sedan. One glance told him that there was nothing remarkable about it except that it was very big and very powerful. He was disappointed. He had been hoping to find some interesting little gadgets attached to it.

As he walked away the G-man who had come down the path with him heard him say, 'Must have some cars for day work, others for night time.' But it didn't mean a thing to him.

The other squad men came out to meet him. Cheyenne asked, 'You got a general broadcast to look out for dark men, not ʝlonds?' They nodded. He said, 'I'll explain all that later. Meanwhile, what about the girl?'

A G-man said, 'We're expecting a homicide squad along any time now. Then we'll know what killed her.'

Cheyenne said, impatiently, 'No, not the stiff. The other girl. Where is she? October Raine?' And then the four squad men stood and stared at him, until one spoke.

'There's no girl here. Only the corpse. We haven't seen another girl at all.'

Cheyenne tore into the house and started to search for the girl, but she wasn't there. And then seemingly hundreds of police suddenly arrived in cars, and the place was thronged with blue-uniformed men.

He got away and started to examine the surroundings for footprints, and then he found one on the path that led up through the trees. He tried to track her, but so many people had run up and down that pathway that except for the first few footprints he didn't see any other signs of her.

He came back to the house in time to hear the police surgeon's pronouncement. 'There'll have to be an autopsy, of course. But there are no wounds or injuries that could have caused death. It seems to me that the girl died from heart failure due to shock.'

Everybody looked at that cable leading to a power pack. Then Cheyenne said, 'Better issue a call to pick up Joe Gell on a possible charge of murder. Looks like he did this. I'll give you his description.'

When that was done he told everyone to look out for October Raine, and he gave her description, too. One of the G-men said, 'You think she's come to harm?'

Cheyenne nodded slowly. 'How else explain her absence? Get everybody to comb these woods and see if there's any trace of her.'

In his mind he was eliminating suspects. It couldn't be the Blond Boys. They had been far ahead of her when she left the house. And he didn't think it could be Joe Gell, because from what he had heard of the former film producer, and what he knew of the resolute girl, he guessed she could hold her own against him. So there was only one other possible suspect.

The man without a face. It made Cheyenne's blood freeze to think of it. But it seemed the only reasonable explanation. October must have come up into the woods after him . . . and walked into the arms of that faceless, mewing monstrosity.

So he gave a third order. 'Find a man without a face. And if you see him . . . don't let him get away!'

10

The search

They didn't find the girl, they didn't find Joe Gell, and the man without a face wasn't to be seen, either. But the police did find that stolen car from Cliff Bottom farm.

It was discovered abandoned in a copse off the road less than five miles from the lakeside village. Later they found a motorist in a ditch with a hole in his head. They had swapped cars and got away in the second one. After that there was no clue. The Blond Boys had disappeared again.

Cheyenne returned to New York. His job was to round up the Blond Boys, and he guessed that by now the gang would be back in their usual haunts. He was also working hard on equipping police cars with a handy little unit that the F.B.I. laboratory had designed for him.

As he explained to the chief, 'When gangs find a winning technique they go on usin' it. That's why we always catch 'em. They go on once too often. Well, the next time the Blond Boys strike, we'll fix 'em. And by God I wish they would strike!'

The chief said, 'You'd better keep your plans quiet this time. Don't forget that big mouth down at Fourth Precinct.'

Cheyenne shrugged. 'He's been traced. Just a kid. Thought he was tipping off a reporter about new developments in the Blond Gang case. But we didn't get anywhere when we followed up the phone number the cop had used. They must have got windy and abandoned the place . . . an unpleasant little downtown apartment that looked as if it was never used.'

And then, unexpectedly, came a dramatic new development. On the second day after the death of Pet Deganya, a voice was heard speaking on the wavelength used by the New York police . . . the voice of the man who had tried to double-cross the Blond Gang some weeks past.

Joe Gell.

His voice came over weak and tremulous, the voice of a man overwhelmed with self-pity and emotion. He was terrified.

It wasn't true what was being said in the papers and on the air, he declared. 'I didn't kill Pet. I only wanted to hurt her a bit. And she was alive when I left her. She died from shock, but not a shock that I gave her. She died because she saw a man without a face.' A pause, then . . . 'God, you oughta see the fellar! He'd make most people's hearts stop.'

And then he went on in a hysterical gabble. 'I won't die for something I never did! You can't touch me for it. And keep Maurice and his Blond Boys off me. I know Maurice . . . he'll finish me! He wants me because he thinks I killed Pet, and Pet was his girl. But he also wants me for the gold bullion I got from him. Get Maurice, quickly, before he gets me! He'll remember this place I've talked about in time.'

And then an excited cop in the radio

room, taking down everything in short-hand, wrote, 'The leader of the Blond Boys is Malta Maurice, and his gang is the old Italian gang from the Karno Piet district.'

Then Joe Gell went off the air. Police and F.B.I. headquarters looked like disturbed ant heaps in the hours after that. Everybody on the case got together and studied the message.

The chief said, 'Gell's terrified, feels sure that Malta Maurice and his gang will catch up with him and kill him slowly and unpleasantly.'

Cheyenne nodded. 'We also know what the Blond Boys were looking for that day they searched the Gell house. Apart from trying to find the girl, by that time dead, it was gold bullion they were after . . . the bullion they stole in one of their raids. That gold was worth a few hundred grand to them.'

Then reports started to filter in. Malta Maurice and his gang, well-known to the police, weren't in their usual haunts and in fact hadn't been seen around for some days.

'So,' said the chief, 'now what do we do?'

Cheyenne came back later that afternoon with a plan.

'Joe Gell used the police wavelength so that only the police would hear his message. He didn't want Malta Maurice to know what he was tellin' us.'

'So?'

'So let's tell Malta Maurice what kind thoughts Joe Gell entertains for him.'

The chief toyed with a pen. 'Where does all that get us?'

Cheyenne said, 'We've got to round up the Blond Boys. Let's use Joe Gell . . . and the bullion . . . as bait.'

The chief said, 'We don't know where Joe Gell . . . or the bullion . . . is.'

'But Malta Maurice does. Remember what Joe Gell said on the radio . . . 'He'll remember this place I've talked about in time'. Joe Gell must, without thinking, have talked about his present hiding place in previous conversations. If Malta Maurice thinks back to those conversations he'll remember and go there. If we're on hand we'll be able to round 'em

149

up, Joe Gell and all.' And he was thinking: That kid, October; I hope we find her!

The chief nodded sarcastically. 'Fine, fine. All we have to do is be on hand when Maurice walks into the trap. Only, how do we know where to be? We know roughly the direction of that transmitter . . . '

'The Catskills?'

'Or some place between or maybe some place beyond.'

Cheyenne rose. 'My guess is that Joe Gell is hiding very close to his old home. Joe's a clever man, and he'll be very cleverly camouflaged. But we've got to find him, and I propose to do it. I'm going out to the Catskills tonight . . . on my own.'

'What do you want me to do?'

'Move men up to Mendip and along all roads radiating around there. And get those new-equipped cars on the road. When you've done that, give Joe Gell's message to the Press. I want Malta Maurice to start racking his brain.'

The chief reached for a phone. 'If Joe

Gell knew what you were doing, Cheyenne, he'd die of fright.'

Cheyenne said, grimly, 'That'd be a whole lot better than for him to land in Malta Maurice's hands. He'd die suffering . . . a long time . . . with Maurice operating on his double-crossing heart with a stiletto.'

When Cheyenne went down to get a car, there was already considerable activity all over the building and out in the vehicle depot. Men were drawing guns and being briefed, and cars were being readied for a long journey. The new apparatus was also being tested . . .

Cheyenne thought: It looks more like preparation for a war than an attempt to round up a gang of mobsters. But then police work is always a war . . . a war on crime.

Cheyenne took the west road out of New York. It was pretty solid with traffic, and even as close as Mendip he was riding in a procession of cars. For a moment he was puzzled, and then he remembered that it was Friday, and weekend vacationers were just starting out. But the trail up to Gell's old house was deserted again, just as it had been the first time he had come that way . . . with October.

He kept trying not to think about the girl. He was a cop, leading a dangerous life. He liked girls, but that was as far as it went. He wasn't the marrying kind and while he was a G-man he wouldn't ever take a wife. That meant he was going to be a bachelor for a long time.

But all the same he had a soft spot for a pretty girl, and when the girl was as pretty and as bright as this attractive ex-airline hostess the spot was pretty big and very, very soft.

He was concerned for the girl, and had been all these days since her disappearance. He hadn't shown it, because he was too well trained to show his feelings. But he had racked his brains to try to find a solution to the girl's disappearance; he'd lain for hours awake at night hoping against hope that his thoughts would lead him to her. And none had come.

The chief had said, 'Once you weren't sure the girl was on the up-and-up. How d'you know she didn't just run out on you, Cheyenne? How d'you know she isn't in on this game for her own purposes? Maybe with an eye to getting that bullion herself, say?'

And Cheyenne had answered shortly, 'I don't know! But I'll stake my badge on it. And I know she saved my life once, and risked her own in an attempt to let me capture a Blond Boy.'

Even more, in his heart he knew that the girl had developed a liking for him, a liking that wasn't far from something deeper. She'd shown it in little ways, but it had been there. And when a girl is like that she doesn't just disappear from the life of the object of her admiration.

No, Cheyenne was certain that October Raine hadn't just voluntarily walked out of his life. Something had happened to her. And the only thought in his mind was that it must be the man without a face.

His own battered, copper-hued face was grim at the thought, and his hand stole unconsciously towards his shoulder holster. If he met this guy without a face . . . well, maybe the guy wouldn't need a face after that.

He hid the car in some bushes when he was half a mile from the Gell house, then set off to approach the place by a roundabout way through the thick undergrowth.

His Indian woodcraft served him well now. He moved silently, surely, flitting from cover to cover, so that even the birds and small animals in the undergrowth were scarcely aware of his passage.

Finally he came out at a point above the house and crawled forward on his belly so as to look down on it. He knew that police had been left to guard the place until after the delayed inquest, and after a time he saw a patrolman, tunic unbuttoned comfortably in front, go for a bored little walk down to the road and back again.

Cheyenne couldn't imagine Joe Gell to be hiding in some secret room in that house; the place just wasn't big enough for that. So, satisfied on that score, satisfied that Joe Gell wasn't hiding there, he started to look around for some other hiding place.

There didn't seem to be any, not unless Joe Gell had learned to be a squirrel or rabbit. True, the wooded hillside that rose so abruptly back of the house was thick with trees and bushes, but Cheyenne knew that a cordon of police had gone right through it, almost shoulder to shoulder, in an attempt to find clues, and they would for certain have come across any secret hiding place.

Abruptly he began to think of the man without a face.

Where did he live and hide, then? He just couldn't live outside in the open during winter, in spite of what that gabby, goat-bearded old turnip hoer had said. He must have a place somewhere nearby . . .

Cheyenne climbed the hill, still with all caution possible, and when the trees thinned near the summit he looked back down the valley.

There were houses all down the valley road . . . maybe a dozen of them, spread out over a distance of two or three miles.

Of course Joe Gell might be in hiding in any one of them, but Cheyenne had a hunch he wasn't. The police had checked with the local inhabitants already, and it didn't seem likely that anyone would have taken in a man wanted for murder.

Cheyenne walked along the ridge a little way, and then came out on to the path that led down to the Gell house. Here it was open and commanded a good view of all the surrounding country, so he sat down among some knee-high scrub and tried to think things out.

It was getting late, and by now the sun was near to the end of its day's journey. Half an hour and dusk would be upon him. His G-force would be in position, all readied for the night's events . . . if there were to be any.

He realised that depended largely upon himself. If his tip to the Press worked, and Malta Maurice suddenly remembered where he could expect to find Joe Gell, then it was pretty certain he would try to get along for his revenge . . . and the bullion. But the point still was . . . along where?

Obstinately Cheyenne was sure that within close range of where he was sitting was the hiding place of Joe Gell.

Well, if he was going to pick up the trail of Malta Maurice and the Blond Boys, he must first find that hiding place and get into position ahead of their arrival.

He shivered as the evening breeze stole coldly up the hillside. The trees were bending before it and moaning softly, in a way that wasn't pleasant to hear.

He looked round. Over to his left ran a main New York road, the one that led through Mendip. He could see black specks crawling along it, and knew they were homeward-bound cars . . . vacationers returning at the end of their holiday, Just as those earlier had been setting out on theirs.

He saw lights in the distance just springing up. They would be at that pleasant lakeside village. He thought: Before I go back I'd like to stop over at that place for a few days. It looks good for a quiet holiday.

His eyes trailed round to the valley bottom, because he felt sure that when anything developed it would come from that direction. And then his head jerked back and his eyes fixed on something that had been there all the time. His memory started unravelling back, until a knot came into view . . . that little something that had tied up in his brain the first time he had come up this way. Something that had asked to be untied and straightened out, some day.

Something that didn't ring true.

And then he jumped to his feet and went across and looked down at that path, and the questions dinning in his brain were: Where does this path lead, apart from to Gell's back door? And whose feet made it? And then the most important question . . . Why? Why was there a path there at all?

He tried to argue the thing out backwards. First, that Joe Gell had made it recently, while living at his old house. Then he remembered the state the house was in and couldn't believe it. Joe Gell might have camped in the place for a few days, but surely not longer.

And this path had been made over a

greater period than a few days, Cheyenne's eyes told him. It wasn't very much used, and was narrow and overgrown, but obviously it was consistently trodden on by some person or persons.

Not Gell? Then perhaps other people down the valley found it convenient to cut through Gell's place in order to get up to the lake. But even as he raised the theory in his mind, Cheyenne disposed of it. He couldn't remember a well-beaten path around the house and down the front to the road, and if valley people had used the path they would have continued it as far as the highway.

So Cheyenne's thoughts came round again to that unknown quantity . . . the man without a face. He was always hanging around the Gell place, that old man had said, though no one knew why. Must be, thought Cheyenne, his feet had made this pathway.

When he had decided on that point, Cheyenne stopped looking down the mist-hung valley, and instead turned his attention the opposite way. He was thinking: Maybe this path leads to the hideout of that bird . . . the guy without a face. It would be something to know where that was to know what part the man without a face played in this mystery. For it seemed to Cheyenne that in some way he was linked up with all this Gell-Blond Boy business.

He moved cautiously, following the path across the dirt road and into the bushes beyond. The path wound considerably, but seemed to lead pretty directly towards the lake; the ground grew marshy on either side and was thick with willows and swamp trees, and a stink came wafting up to his nostrils as the ooze breathed bad vapour at him.

And then, just when he was thinking he was on a good thing, the path ended in . . . another path!

This was a broader, much more frequented pathway obviously, and it seemed to run all down the creek and out round the bay towards that lakeside village. It was probably a path beaten by the many feet of vacationers. Cheyenne cursed. This put an end to his recent high hopes. He hesitated, not knowing which way to go. Because of the low hanging trees that came almost to the water's edge, he couldn't see very well. It was also coming dark under these gently swaying trees.

He decided to go down towards the main water, and he set off along the path. In a tiny inlet along the way he found three holiday cruisers at anchor. A radio was playing softly and the people were talking across the water to each other. Cheyenne passed quietly on; there didn't seem any future in that crowd.

He found it much the same all down the creek.

Some of the boats out on the water he wasn't so sure of. There was one past the rotting hulk that was part-beached . . . this was a crude barge converted into a houseboat, and had a dilapidated air as it lay anchored out in the stream. There was no sign of life about it, either.

And there was still another curious craft anchored almost where the creek emptied into the lake . . . curious in its air of neglect and desertion. There was no one about. No lights.

Cheyenne pulled himself together, peering through the gloom. So what? It just meant, maybe, that some people didn't paint their boats, didn't look after them well, didn't live on them all the time. And there was nothing criminal in any of that.

He felt despondent. In a matter of minutes it would be dark, and he still hadn't a clue to the hideout of Joe Gell, still didn't know where to expect the Blond Boys when they arrived. If they arrived, that was.

He decided to get back to the top of the hill, so that he could watch all ways and listen for any unusual sounds, and so he started back quickly along the creek pathway.

Round a bend he found himself standing within a yard of a silent man. And the man had a blond head and a deadpan face.

Cheyenne jumped him before he could move. His hands gripped for the throat, found it, and started to squeeze him into unconsciousness. Queer sounds came from that tortured throat . . . and then a knife slashed at Cheyenne's chest. The G-man let go with one hand at that and grabbed the knife-hand, and then the two went rolling into the shallow water, fighting like fury.

It went on for a minute, and Cheyenne knew all the time he was going to lick the fellar. Then the fellar seemed to feel it, too, and was roused to desperation by the thought. He seemed to go mad, and in his frenzy Cheyenne couldn't quite hold him.

He started to pound up at that soft face, to knock the man out, but the blows didn't seem to have effect. Then that knife-hand came loose and Cheyenne saw it streaking for him. He rolled, and kept on rolling, and somehow twisted that hand away . . .

The Blond Boy started to gurgle curiously, and Cheyenne realised that he had rolled on top of the knife. His assailant went limp, though his legs were twitching curiously.

Cheyenne stood up in the water, careful, suspicious of a ruse. But the Blond Boy just lay there twitching and making small mouth noises, so Cheyenne took him by the collar and dragged him on to the path.

That done, Cheyenne looked around. The place was shadowy, the rustling trees breathed menace, but Cheyenne's instinct told him they were alone, so he took out a pencil torch and flashed it on to the face of the Blond Boy.

The eyes were closed. At any rate, he couldn't see them

He knew what to do. He slipped his fingers under that smooth, hairless chin and pulled up and backwards. It seemed as though the skin was coming off . . . even the blond hair. And then something limp hung in Cheyenne's fingers.

He shone the light on it with satisfaction. It was cleverly done . . . a mask moulded out of a soft, porous rubber that fitted completely over the head. Cheyenne didn't need to examine it closely to know what the material was composed of, or how it was made, with real hair fixed on to the scalp. He slipped it into his pocket.

Instead he turned his light casually on

to the face of his assailant . . . and got the shock of his life!

For there was no face on that dead body . . . there'd been no face under the mask at all!

11

The end of Joe Gell

Cheyenne crouched there on that dark pathway, his light on the corpse. Because he knew now that it was a corpse beneath him, knew it without feeling for the heart or pulse.

And he tried to work things out. He was bewildered. For one awful second he wondered if he was wrong, if in fact all those Blond Boys wore masks to cover their lack of faces. And then he said, 'Bah!' The thought was too fantastic.

The only other thought that came to him was, 'Well, then, it looks like the man without a face has joined the Blond Boys.' But somehow that theory didn't fit, either.

He pulled the corpse into the under-growth, and searched through the pockets. There was nothing in them at all. So back he came on to the path and crouched down again and waited.

Now he knew that he was near to Joe Gell, knew that if Malta Maurice remembered where Joe Gell might be, sooner or later he would come along this path trodden by the first Blond Boy . . . the man without a face.

It wasn't good, sitting there and thinking of that faceless thing only a few yards back of him in the bush. If he turned his head he could see the dark shape of it lying there, only Cheyenne didn't turn his head. He knew it was a corpse and corpses didn't worry him.

But he still couldn't help thinking about that face.

Just a flat rawness, like a face that has been burnt off. With a small hole for a mouth, and smaller holes for nostrils. Thinking back, Cheyenne couldn't remember if the thing had eyes at all. He hadn't noticed any.

The hours passed. He squatted there patiently, unmindful of discomfort and the slow passing of time. If necessary he'd stay there till dawn.

But all the same it was quite a bit

before midnight when he heard sounds. Only they came from the water, from down the creek. It was a launch, big and powerful; Cheyenne got the outline against some star-reflecting water that wasn't shadowed by overhanging trees. It was stealing silently along the creek, engines scarcely making a sound.

Cheyenne jerked erect. This was a turn of events that he hadn't foreseen, that his men might approach by boat. And still the question rang in his brain . . . approach where?

The engines cut, fifty yards away, and the launch came gliding up in complete silence now. It was without navigation lights, and there was no sign of life aboard.

Then Cheyenne thought that he had been spotted, for the launch had turned towards the dark shore and seemed to be heading straight for him. A few seconds later he realised that it was a trick of the half-light; the launch was coming ashore at the bend below him.

He slipped down the pathway, hands outstretched to ward off the low tree branches and trailing thorns. Just round this bend the old, half-beached hulk lay on its side. He saw the launch bump gently against it, then a dark figure sprang aboard the hulk and started to tie up. Now Cheyenne saw plenty of movement as half a dozen or more shadowy shapes leapt on to the hulk.

When he saw how many there were, he felt satisfied. It seemed the bait had pulled, and the trap was about to close on the men he wanted.

There was just the trouble of that launch. Cheyenne wanted, if possible, to immobilise it before he gave the signal for a close in by his ring of waiting men. But that might take some doing. He also couldn't yet see the object of this manoeuvre in tying up to the hulk.

He crept nearer. The men were whispering. Just then a thin yellow slice of moon rode clear of a cloudbank that had come up with night. Cheyenne saw a deadpan face . . . and another, and another. They were his men all right.

But they were doing something to the tumbledown deckhouse, to a door on it.

There was a splintering sound, as if wood was being prized apart.

Somewhere someone started to shout, and Cheyenne realised that it was coming from within the hulk. Someone was inside that old ruin. It was something he had never considered, that anyone could be aboard. He had thought it to be filled with stagnant water . . .

Suddenly the door must have been torn open, for it swung back and yellow lamplight seemed to blaze with blinding brilliance into his eyes. At once the shouting grew louder, and Cheyenne, crawling forward on his stomach, realised that it was high-pitched in terror . . . so high that for a moment he thought it to be a woman's.

Three or four men dropped down through the deckhouse. The others stood on guard over the launch and hulk.

Cheyenne decided that he was going to be very lucky if he managed to reach the launch, as he had wanted.

That terrified voice screamed up to him. He didn't need to be told that it was Joe Gell's, that Malta Maurice had remembered Joe Gell at some time mentioning this beached hulk he owned.

Then he remembered the blond mask that he had taken from off the man without a face, and it gave him an idea. He hated the thought, hated the idea of having that thing on his face after it had covered that hideous faceless head. But it went on.

He came silently through the shadows now until he was by the sloping deck of the hulk, and no one saw him approach. Then he waited for the moon to come out before making his next move.

And all the time Joe Gell was yelling below.

Cheyenne thought, 'Nice guy, Maurice!' Gell had probably been literally right in saying that Malta Maurice would take his heart out if he caught up with him!

Joe Gell was shouting, 'I didn't do it, Maurice. Didn't kill Pet. I wouldn't have done. Keep 'em away from me — I tell you, I didn't do anything to her. It was a guy without a face. He just looked at her and her heart went.'

Someone snarled, 'The hell, you pick likely stories.'

And then the moon came out, and Cheyenne moved. He lifted his head to the light, so that he was plain to be seen, and then he clambered slowly up the deck towards where the sentries were grouped together. They stopped talking the moment he started to come up to them.

Then they must have seen his deadpan face, for a voice exploded quietly, 'I thought we'd gotten visitors! The hell, how many are up on deck, anyway?'

Cheyenne growled something and nothing, and went to where the doorway showed yellow against the dark night sky. He glanced down. Saw a largish, quite well-furnished saloon. On a table in a corner was a pretty impressive radio installation. That would be Joe Gell's short wave transmitter, Cheyenne thought.

Then he saw Joe Gell, and recognised him as the man he had seen crouching over Pet Deganya's body that day.

They'd got Joe's fat, soft body and bent him backwards over a water barrel. His fat white face was staring up in agony, straight into Cheyenne's eyes.

Two deadpan Blond Boys had torn his shirt open in front, revealing unhealthy, white fatness over his ribs and middle.

Gell's voice screamed out, 'It's true. It's a fellar got burnt in a movie fire. He was the operator. His face was so bad they couldn't do anything with it, and people couldn't look at him. He went half-crazed, then he remembered a film I'd made . . . one he'd screened. About a plastic surgeon. Only it was all fake, done with some moulded rubber . . . '

'He's telling us,' said Maurice in disgust. 'Don't we know? Didn't you fit us up, too?'

Gell went on talking, trying desperately to keep that knifepoint away from his heart. 'He came and lived out here, waiting for me to come back from Hollywood, as he guessed I would. That day the cops found Pet he came here carrying a girl he'd picked up . . . '

Cheyenne went rigid, not daring to move lest he miss a word of Gell's talk.

'He was stark crazy, violent. He'd have

killed me if I'd have refused to help him. So I did. I gave him my mask, the one I used on raids when I was operating the transmitter.'

They were all listening, up there on deck. Now Cheyenne felt a movement. A man had turned, was looking towards him. Then came a whisper, and Cheyenne cursed, knowing what it meant.

One of the men had remembered his sudden appearance, remembered his suspicions of the time. Now those suspicions had been revived by Joe Gell's shouted gabble from below.

The man who had whispered had probably said, 'Is that guy one of us, him standing by the hatchway, or is he this guy without a face?'

At this moment Cheyenne abandoned all ideas of trying to get aboard the launch to immobilise it. Now he must get away far enough to be able to give the signal for the net to start to close. Maybe he should have kept clear of this hulk in the first place, he thought; he should have made sure of triggering off that warning. Then he decided that what he had learned was worth the risk. Now he had to get away . . .

The man who had whispered came clambering down the sloping deck towards the lighted hatchway. When he reached it he looked down. Cheyenne knew he was counting.

It was at that moment that Malta Maurice stopped playing with Gell and started in to work. Suddenly he slashed.

'Now, where's that bullion?' snarled Malta.

But even in his agony Joe Gell . . . Gell the man who couldn't stand pain, Gell the coward . . . had sense to realize that if he did give up that secret, then for certain Malta Maurice would go to work with his knife.

Joe was screaming, 'I won't tell you . . . won't tell you at all if you don't let up!'

The deadpan who was counting started to turn.

Then Cheyenne knew the game was up, so he kicked that deadpan just behind the knee, and that shot the Blond Boy face first down the hatchway, shouting even before he landed on top of the prostrate Joe Gell.

Even as he turned to run, Cheyenne saw something else.

A mop of blonde hair . . . October . . . Jumping as if from some hiding place on to Malta Maurice's back.

He groaned. Why the heck couldn't she have remained hidden a second longer! As it was, he couldn't go down to help her. She must take what came.

All this flashed through his mind in the fraction of a second as he started to roll down the sloping deck. He hit the dry mud foreshore just as hell broke loose on the hulk.

The remaining deadpans got their guns up and laced the night with fire, and one was a tommy gun. Below deck was a lot of frenzied excitement, then Malta Maurice's voice raised in furious anger.

And then came a scream and Cheyenne didn't know the owner of it, Joe Gell . . . or the girl!

He went diving behind some tree roots before the tommy quite swept round to him, then he went away into the darkness on his belly. When he was far enough away to be safe from a bullet, he sat up and clipped a little device on to his gun barrel, pointed it upwards and fired. The bullet sped off into the dark, followed more slowly by something that lobbed up to a height of maybe a couple of hundred feet before softly exploding and starring out into a drooping red fern of light, brilliant in that blackness.

Almost at once Cheyenne heard the launch roar into life.

The gang had panicked and were getting away. He saw a shaft of light stab out as the forward searchlight went on to help them negotiate the narrow creek, and he ran to the water's edge to take a bang at them. He removed that damp, clinging mask and felt better.

He fired three times in quick succession, and someone cried out in pain. Then he tried to do a worm act as lead came spitting viciously over the water towards him. The launch roared out into the lake. So far they had got away again.

Along the shore, close by the lights of the lakeside village, car headlights blinked out a signal, and the launch's headlight answered back. Cheyenne nodded in the dark, as if not wholly unpleased about something, then turned and raced along the path towards the hulk.

The lamp still cast its yellow light out into the night sky, and provided a beacon for him. He clambered up the sloping deck again, and looked below.

Joe Gell stared up at him, still sprawled back across that barrel. He was quite dead.

There was a blonde head face down just below him. Cheyenne dropped into the saloon and knelt by her side. There was a bruise across her forehead, as if someone had clipped her with a gun barrel. She was out, but alive and would soon recover.

She was stirring as he picked her up and hoisted her across his shoulder before clambering up the ladder. When the cool night air hit her she started to struggle, tried to get away from him, moaning.

Cheyenne stopped and let her down on to her feet but he still kept his arms round her to support her. He said, 'It's all right, honey. It's me, Cheyenne Charlie. You're quite safe . . . '

'Cheyenne?' There was a sob of relief in her voice. He felt her hands grip frantically into him, as if to make sure it was the G-man. 'Thank god you came, Cheyenne! For a moment I thought I was on his back again . . . that creature without a face. I don't think my dreams will ever be free from that awful shock, of seeing that face when I came to . . . '

The special operator was supporting her but walking rapidly up the path, flashing his torch for guidance. When they passed the place where the faceless corpse lay, he kept his light to one side so that the girl wouldn't see it in all its horror.

He said, urgently, 'You've got to keep up with me, October, otherwise I'll just have to leave you. The Blond Boys have got away in a boat, and I want to be in on the death when they run into a trap I've laid.'

She started running. 'You won't get away from me this time,' she said emphatically. 'I'm not going to be left in the dark around this place.'

They crossed the dirt road and started to go down among the dark, whispering spruce and larch trees. As they scrambled down the steep path, she found words to explain how things happened.

'I tried to follow you up this path. I thought you must have gone across the dirt road into the swamp, so I ran after you. Suddenly there was that man again, right in front of me. It was so horrible, so terrifying, I think I must have fainted.

'Next thing I knew I was in that boat. Joe Gell had arrived not much before me, to find that the man without a face had been camping in the boat, waiting for him to return from Hollywood. The man was mad, stark, staring mad. He terrified Joe as much as he frightened me. And the way he talked, like a cat mewing through that little mouth of his . . . but we could understand him.

'He wanted a rubber face because the plastic surgeons couldn't do anything to his own. Joe gave him one of the masks he had made for the Blond Gang.'

Cheyenne nodded. He didn't tell the girl that the mask was in his pocket, and the late owner was dead, killed in a fight with the F.B.I. man.

'What happened to you, all the time you were there? Did they . . . hurt you?'

She whispered, 'No. Joe didn't want me to be harmed. I think his idea was that if he looked well after me it would be in his favour if he got caught by the police. So he kept the madman off and looked rather well after me, though he kept me a prisoner.'

Cheyenne said, 'I'm surprised at Joe being able to face up to the madman. How come?'

'It was an accident. Joe suddenly realised that he could make the madman quiet simply by saying, 'When that mask wears out I won't make you another'.'

Cheyenne started to laugh. She said, indignantly, 'It may sound comical and childish, but you should have seen it work. Every time Joe said that the madman used to cringe in a corner and say he was sorry, he would do everything Joe told him to do. You know, I think for once in his life Joe felt happy. For once he'd found someone who was afraid of him and treated him with respect.'

Cheyenne helped her down a steep grade. 'Thank God for that. It was a lucky break for you, October.' She didn't answer; she didn't need to.

He shouted as they came down to the house, and a suspicious cop came out the back way waving a powerful torch.

Cheyenne came staggering in, holding the girl upright. His F.B.I. badge came out and quieted the suspicions of the patrolman. Quickly Cheyenne gave some word of explanation. At once the cop said, 'We got an alert on the phone when your star shell went up. Then we got another call from Long Lake village, sayin' some gunnies had landed off a launch and had got away in a big, fast car. There was some shootin' as they went through the village . . . '

Cheyenne interrupted. 'What colour of a car did you say it was?'

The cop said, promptly, 'I didn't. But it was yellow, the report said.'

Cheyenne patted the girl on her shoulder as if pleased with her or with something. 'That's good,' he said approvingly. 'So now they think we're hunting for a mob of blond-haired, deadpan gunnies ridin' around in a big yellow car.'

The cop stared. 'Well, aren't we?'

Cheyenne started for the door. 'Not on your life.' But he didn't say any more and went out the front way. October, who seemed to have recovered quickly, trotted by his side.

He told her she ought to stay behind with the cops, but he knew it was useless. October felt comfort in nobody's presence but his own.

It was flattering, but that didn't prevent Cheyenne from going as hard as he could for his car, hidden back along the road. 'You can get all the rest you require once you're in it,' he told her, in answer to her pleas for a slower pace.

But they reached it eventually, October sobbing her thankfulness. There was food and drink in the back, and when she had recovered sufficiently she opened the case and fed Cheyenne as he drove. The drink came wonderfully refreshing to them . . . and it wasn't coke, either.

When they reached Mendip, suddenly

they were among traffic again. There was a lot of it, homeward bound, for the most part. Just car after car streaking along the concrete in an effort to reach at least the western suburbs of New York before midnight.

Cheyenne turned the wheel and sped against the stream of traffic. The way he was going, there were not many other cars and he was able to open out and keep up a high speed, though dazzled by the never-ending string of headlights approaching.

He explained, 'I might be wrong, but I've got a hunch those birds will try to brazen their way to New York tonight. After all, their disguise has always got them past the police before ... they'll argue, why not tonight, too? So I'm hoping to get to the roadblock up the way here in time for the kill. They had to go a long way round, remember, first up the lake, then round on to the main highway past Long Lake village. Maybe we'll be in time.'

October sat snuggling close to him at his side. She said, 'You're so clever,

G-man. You think of everything, don't you?'

Complacently, grinning to himself in the dark, he said, 'Sure, now, I do get a few hunches right once in a while.'

So then she asked, almost maliciously, 'All right, big boy, now tell me . . . where's that gold bullion?'

His foot came off the accelerator. 'You know?' he demanded.

'I know,' she returned. 'And if you don't, then you're a dumb cluck who should never return to California.'

She heard him say meekly, 'Then I'm a dumb cluck, honey.'

12

Black light

He was slowing now, because there was an illuminated Police barrier just ahead. They were the only car to approach from the east side, but westward was a line of fuming motorists which must have stretched at least a quarter of a mile back. Cheyenne looked at it and then said, 'They won't have got through yet, not with that amount of traffic having to be examined.'

He pulled off the road, then got out with the girl. As they walked across to the block he said, 'You'll have to tell me all about that gold bullion, honey. It'd look well in my report. Where is it? In the hulk?'

She shook her head. Cheyenne introduced himself to the police captain in charge of the roadblock, then walked across to where a police car was parked on the verge, so that its unlighted headlamps covered the road immediately in front of the barrier. Cheyenne listened, heard the engine running and something like a generator whining, and was satisfied.

He stood back and watched the procedure. There were a dozen uniformed patrolmen close about that barrier. Some carried riot guns at the ready, and others wore walkie-talkie sets. Each car out of that long line was made to approach the barrier slowly then stop, right in front of those lightless headlamps of the stationary patrol car.

The patrolmen made a check on the occupants, then let them through.

Cheyenne thought: And all this is happening on every road within a fifteen-mile radius of Mendip. He couldn't see how the gang could get away this time . . . not unless they ditched their escape car and split up and trickled through the net harmlessly that way, in ones and twos. He didn't think they would do that. They would still have confidence in the disguise that had brought them to safety so many times before; for they wouldn't know that Cheyenne Charlie had seen through it just as he had tumbled to those deadpan masks of theirs, and was now able to detect it.

He walked down the line of cars. Most were big cars many with six, seven or more male occupants. Looking at them Cheyenne could imagine any bunch to be the mob he was after . . . at times like these every man looked much of a crook.

The captain and the girl had walked after him. The captain said, 'There ain't a big yellow car in the whole line of traffic.'

Cheyenne retorted, 'There might be one when they get up to that barrier.' He asked, 'Has there been a sports event locally?' He indicated the many cars with their all-male occupants. 'I never knew men liked travelling together in bunches, like bananas. Me, I always like to have girls with me.'

October slipped her arm through his, smiled, 'Like now?'

The captain told them, 'There was a race meeting. Maybe that accounts for all these fellars travelling together. It makes it harder for us.'

'But easier for the Blond Boys,' added Cheyenne.

They went back to the barrier. Cheyenne had got his eye on one big black car, packed full of blue-chinned huskies. It didn't look much different from other cars, but all the same there was something about it that aroused his suspicions. Perhaps it was that the men lolling inside were too elaborately bored and unconcerned by police activity.

Cheyenne said to the girl, 'You see our car, parked back there? You go an' plonk yourself inside and don't stir, get me?'

'You think something's going to happen?'

Cheyenne looked at that big black car. As yet he had nothing but suspicions. But in a minute or so . . .

He said, 'Don't talk, but get moving. And this time don't come runnin' after me.' He took the gun out of his shoulder holster and slipped it into his coat pocket. He didn't take his hand off the butt kept it there inside his pocket.

It handicapped him, having his hand

there. When he was assaulted a second later, only one arm was there to protect him from October. She had her arms round him, scandalizing the police captain. She was kissing him affectionately, as if she had been used to kissing him for many a year.

Cheyenne watched that approaching car, saw it was still a minute or two away from the barrier, and submitted meekly.

At last the girl let go. She sighed, 'That was nice. You're a comforting boy friend to have, Cheyenne.'

Cheyenne cracked, 'It's the comparison that does it. You never looked twice at my battered face until you saw that gent without one. It made me seem quite handsome.'

She shook her head. 'You're going a bit far there, Cheyenne. Even your mother couldn't have thought that about you.'

He sent her scooting to the security of their car, then stood to one side from the barrier.

A Pontiac was allowed through. There was only one other car before that big, black, suspicious-looking vehicle.

Cheyenne heard one of the lugs in the

black car call out,

'What're you lookin' for, bub? If it's Rita Hayworth, she'll most likely be down Reno way.'

It was just a bit too jolly, too forced. Cheyenne wasn't missing a thing. Some cop yapped off his big mouth,

'We're looking for a yaller car, wise guy. You ain't got no yaller car wid you, have you?'

Cheyenne heard a voice float out, 'Let's us out, I guess. Never seen a yellar car look as black as this of ours.'

They'd be very confident, of course, hearing all that. Sitting in a big black car when the cops were looking for a yellow one. And they'd be looking for blond men. too, they'd be thinking.

That other car was given the clear and went accelerating violently, demonstrating the annoyance . . . or could it be relief? . . . of the driver.

The big black car crept up to the barrier. A big black car from bonnet to tail light. Creeping up.

A big black car with a yellow bonnet, Cheyenne saw.

A big black car that was going mostly yellow, he realised, and the gun started to lift out of his pocket.

Then that big black car was standing right in the beam of black light from the stationary patrol car, and it was as yellow as any car Cheyenne had ever seen. He heard the police captain gasp at his side, saw the patrolmen with riot rifles lift them.

Someone else must have seen the yellowing bonnet . . . the driver of that big car. Cheyenne heard a shout and a curse, and then the car whirled swiftly, accelerating, trying to make a complete turn in the wide road. But failing.

Guns belted off, and glass shattered. The roar of that accelerating engine filled the night air like the bellow of a wounded bull. All down the long line of stationary traffic men dived out of their vehicles and took cover from the flying lead in the deepest ditch they could find.

Guns flamed from the car, trying to reverse before going ahead again. A cop went down, rifle clattering. Cheyenne grabbed his rifle and ran forward.

Some damn' fool decided to switch on his headlights, and that put the G-man in the full beam as he doubled across the road. He pumped off a couple of rounds from his side, then felt lead zipping close to him and let fly at those offending lights. He must have hit something or somebody, for they went out.

Then the car went forward, bumping along the rough edge of the road. The rifle fire hotted up, and the back of that car must have been a lot of perforated metal by now.

Then it caught on fire and came to a halt. The flames shot up, with a roaring sound that was like a train suddenly entering a tunnel. Men came tumbling out . . . but not seven of them . . . three or four, and they were staggering and hurt.

The others were trapped inside, and Cheyenne could hear them crying for help.

That was the trouble . . . help couldn't get to them with those other gunmen trying desperately to fight back against the police.

The police came running forward,

firing. Lead kept hitting the gunmen, tearing into their flesh, but they fought on with the viciousness of cornered rats who know that death is inevitable if captured, anyway. They were going out, and they wanted to do as much damage to hurt as much as possible, before the curtain came down for them.

Cheyenne was pretty near by now, coming up from behind the blazing vehicle. He saw one dark-haired gunman go down in a twitching huddle of limbs, saw a second spin round, drop to his knees and still keep on firing. So he pumped off a round and shattered the gunnies shoulder and put him out of the fight.

The last gunman . . . Cheyenne hoped it was Malta Maurice, but didn't know . . . came jumping round at him then. His gun was empty and he hurled it at the G-man, then tried to pick up a revolver that had fallen from another gunnie's hand.

Cheyenne tried to stop him by kicking into him, and both went down. The firing stopped. A man inside that blazing car gave a last cry. Cheyenne wanted to take the last surviving gunnie alive, but he wasn't taking risks all the same.

He found himself being tripped going down. Saw that snarling, Latin face somewhere down among his feet saw a revolver coming up.

There wasn't time for niceties. 'Him or me!' thought Cheyenne, jabbing the rifle muzzle into that open mouth. He pulled the trigger a second ahead of the gunnie. The gunnie's bullet took part of an eyebrow off. But that didn't matter. At least he still had a head, and that gunnie at his feet . . . well, he didn't have one at all.

Cheyenne got to his feet and looked around. The cop captain came running up with his men. Cheyenne said, 'It's all over. You c'n pick up the bits now.' He looked at the line of traffic. 'If those drivers aren't too bogged down in the ditch you c'n let 'em go home to thrill their wives with this story.'

He walked across to his car. October opened the door. When she saw the blood on his face she cried out with alarm then switched on the interior light and cleaned his face for him.

When that was done, Cheyenne took another drink then said, 'I'm going back to New York to make my report. You comin' with me?'

October nodded. 'New York sounds fine after these wide open spaces,' she said. 'I've had enough thrills to last me a long time. Maybe I'll go back to films or being an air-hostess — '

Cheyenne started the engine. 'Before you do,' he said anxiously 'just help a fellar by hintin' where that bullion is hidden.'

Her reply startled him. 'It's in the house. You should know. I'm betting you saw it when I did.'

'Oh yeah? I don't remember seein' any gold bullion. Whereabouts in the house would it be, d'you reckon?'

'In the library.'

'But, holy gee, that room hadn't been opened in years. There was that dust an' those cobwebs. It couldn't have been . . . '

October sighed. 'For once I'm one up on a G-man. Who'd have thought it!' Then she went on . . . 'if you'd ever worked in films you wouldn't be talking like that. It was too much . . . too overdone. Done in the best Hollywood style. That was my first thought. Those cobwebs were phoney. I guess they make 'em when they're needed in films.'

Cheyenne said, 'I'm beginning to get it. Why don't I keep remembering that Joe Gell was a film producer! Of course he could build up that room to look like anything he wanted . . . such as a room that hadn't been entered for years. Well. I'm not the only one that was taken in. Malta Maurice and his pals didn't suspect either.'

October said, 'Joe Gell was a clever man. He did most things brilliantly. And I feel a soft spot for the slug because he protected me from the madman all those awful days.'

'You still haven't told me where I'd find the gold in that library.' They were roaring through the silent deserted main street of Mendip now; soon they'd be in New York.

'You saw that shelf collapse as if rotten? Collapse under the weight of of those old books. Have a look at those books. I'll make a guess they're cast gold . . . solid gold. With a leather cover stuck to them to make them look like books. That's why they were in that bottom shelf, I guess. Joe Gell wouldn't lift heavy weights any higher than he could help. When people started banging about it must have been the last straw and that overloaded shelf cracked under the strain.'

Cheyenne was watching her out of the corner of his eye. He said, 'You're a smart kid. Take my tip and don't go back to being an air-hostess. The F.B.I. need smart people, even in the sten department. After my report maybe they'll find a lot more special jobs for you to go on.'

She shuddered and crept close to him. 'Just now I don't feel like anything more exciting than straight stenography. But . . . I'll think about it.'

A couple of miles down the road she came out of her thoughts to say, 'But that wasn't so smart, guessing about those gold bricks. You're far smarter, Cheyenne. Honest, you're the smartest guy I know. When you guess it's a cert.'

Cheyenne just grinned. It was nice to

hear such compliments from a girl as pretty as October Raine.

She went on, 'But I still don't get it. We were looking for a yellow car, but instead you only looked at black ones. And that big black car . . . I was watching. I saw it gradually turn yellow at the barrier. It was like magic.'

'It was black magic, honey. Black light, anyway.' Cheyenne stood on the accelerator now on the broad several-lined New York highway. He was in a hurry to get home. 'I knew that a car couldn't change from yellow to black easily, yet every report we got of the Blond Boys escaping after one of their raids suggested that in a space of seconds they were able to change the yellow colour of their car for some other.

'It gave me an idea. I thought maybe the car paint was treated with some pigment that reacts to ultra violet light. If that were so, a few ultra-violet ray lamps fixed to the wings and roof could turn that car yellow by the touch of a switch . . . or black or its normal colour when the ultra violet light was turned off.

'That patrol car that was parked by the barrier was throwing out a beam of ultra violet light through one of its headlamps. You can't see it, ultra violet . . . which is why it's sometimes called black light. But the moment that car came in front of the beam it was revealed as the yellow car we were after.'

October sighed. 'You're wonderful. How did you think all that out?'

Cheyenne grinned. 'Keep saying I'm clever. I like to hear it. But . . . you know where I got that idea from? From vaudeville. They've had quite a few black light acts lately. So . . . am I still as clever as you thought?'

She whispered, 'You won't be so clever if you must go straight on and make your report. Can't you see I'm crazy about you, you pug-faced old G-man!'

So he stopped the car. Not because he resented allusions to his face but because a report could wait, anyway. And a bonny girl like October Raine . . . well, she mightn't.

THE END

Other titles in the
Linford Mystery Library:

THE FLUTTERING

David Whitehead

Something terrifying has started happening in Eggerton. People are turning up drained of blood and very, very dead. Have vampire bats started attacking humans? If so, then who's delivering the hammer-blow that finally kills the victims? For Detective Inspector Jack Sears it's a mystery that not even virologist Doctor Christopher Deacon can fathom. But then the police get lucky. Against all the odds one of the victims survives. But strangely enough, that's when things go from bad to worse . . .